GODDESS

GODDESS

Bloomsbury Publishing, London, New Delhi, New York and Sydney

First published in Great Britain in April 2014 by Bloomsbury Publishing Plc
50 Bedford Square, London WC1B 3DP

A CIP catalogue record for this book is available from the British Library

ISBN 978 1 4088 1526 7

Typeset by Hewer Text UK Ltd, Edinburgh
Printed and bound in Great Britain by CPI Group (UK) Ltd, Croydon CR0 4YY

1 3 5 7 9 10 8 6 4 2

www.bloomsbury.com

For my Reagan cousins:
Robbie, John, Jane and Will,
and all their wonderful family

'Goddess of Woods, tremendous in the chase
To the mountain boars and all the savage race!
Look upon us on earth! Unfold our fate,
And say what region is our destined seat?
Where shall we next thy lasting temples raise?
And choirs of virgins celebrate thy praise?'

The prayer of Brutus, Prince of Troy and first king of
Britain, to the goddess Artemis.

From Geoffrey of Monmouth's
History of the Kings of Britain, c.1136

PROLOGUE

When I was a little girl, I tried to imagine what it would be like if the gods spoke to us as they did in ancient times. I imagined it would sound like the rush of wind in trees, or a ripple of silver bells.

The call of the goddess was different. Hounds howled in my head and snapped at my heels; I felt their teeth as my own voice was torn from me.

I woke to the taste of blood.

CHAPTER 1

The night my life was fated to change forever began with flowers, and ended with snakes.

The flowers were a bunch of carnations thrown at my feet. 'Goddess save you, dearie!' cried the fat old woman who'd tossed them. 'May Holy Artemis bless your sweet face!'

Not that she could actually see it, of course. Hand-maidens and priestesses of the Cult of Artemis are veiled in public. Today, in honour of the festival, we were in full ancient Greek costume – silk robes, fur pelts and floral garlands. The spectators who'd lined the streets of London to watch the procession would expect nothing less.

'Make the most of it,' said Callisto as she walked beside me. 'You need all the blessings you can get.'

I decided to keep my dignity and not rise to the bait. I could tell Cally was wearing her best holy expression beneath the veil and was annoyed that no one could see it. She was probably imagining how good it would have looked on the giant TV screens outside the temple, which would broadcast the ceremony to the waiting crowd.

Britain is officially a secular country but Artemis's image is stamped on every pound coin, and her crescent moon shines from the top right-hand corner of the Union Jack. Once a month, and on festival days, our High Priestess gives an oracle from the goddess. The words of the prophecies are always riddling, but trying to make sense of the predictions gives people comfort, especially in difficult times. That Festival Day the future felt particularly uncertain. The country was still reeling from the financial crash and the disaster of foreign wars, and months of strikes and rioting. The hope in people's faces was more like hunger as they watched us climb the temple steps.

The Temple of Artemis sits at the top of Ludgate Hill, the highest point of the City of London. Nowadays it's hemmed in by skyscrapers and tower blocks, and it doesn't dominate the skyline as it once did. But it's still an icon. The best view is from the Southbank, looking across the Thames to where the dome rises up from the city like a pale moon.

The temple was rebuilt in the seventeenth century and is beginning to show its age. The marble is chipped, the bronze is dented and the gold leaf is wearing thin. But the Sacred Hall is still a kaleidoscope of gilded arches and glittering mosaics, and the ten-foot statue of the goddess still makes tourists gawp.

That is the public temple. The private temple is underneath, and was just a bare stone room in the crypt. All it contains is King Brutus's altar stone. Very few people are allowed in here, and only priestesses may draw back the curtain across the threshold to see what lay behind, the Chamber of the Oracle. It holds a statue of Artemis that is said to have been saved from the ruins of Troy. In under two weeks' time, when I turned sixteen and was initiated as a priestess, I would pass through the curtain and see the image for the first time. There was a shiver in the pit of my stomach whenever I thought of it.

Today was my sixteenth Festival of the Goddess. My first was at just six months old, a baby left on the temple steps. It's always felt special: the long hushed day of fasting and prayer leading to the moment when the temple doors swing open to welcome us, their bronze panels gleaming in the last of the evening light.

Inside, the air was scented with lilies and incense. Candlelight glimmered on jewel-coloured glass and gold, and you could hardly see the altar for the wilderness of flowers heaped around it. Opis, our High Priestess, was standing on the dais. She's a small woman, but slim and upright, with a moonstone headdress crowning her long black hair. She doesn't wear a veil because she is the oracle, and therefore the goddess's human face.

For as long as I can remember, I've dreamed of standing in Opis's place, feeling the weight of the diadem on my head and the breath of the goddess on my skin. It's Cally's dream too. But for now the two of us took our places beside the altar with the rest of the cult. Seven handmaidens and eight priestesses joined together in the choral song:

> 'Hail to thee, maiden blest,
> Proudest and holiest:
> God's daughter, great in bliss,
> Leto-born, Artemis . . .'

To the clash of cymbals, Opis lifted up her arms, and a huge beaten-silver disc rose from behind the altar, dappling the temple with reflected light. At the same time, the blue-painted ceiling of the dome burst into a bright scatter of stars. The congregation joined the hymn, hailing the goddess by her two titles: Artemis Theron, Queen of Beasts, and Artemis Selene, Lady of the Moon.

This was the cue for Opis to narrate our founding story. Brutus, Prince of Troy, is wandering in exile after his city's downfall. He finds a ruined temple to Artemis, where the goddess appears to him in a dream. She tells him to lead his followers to the island of Albion, which Brutus is to rename after himself. There he and his men battle the monstrous Gogmagoc and win the land of Britain for their own.

'. . . coming to the river Thames, Brutus walked along the shore, and at last pitched upon a place very fit for his purpose. Here, therefore, he built a city, which he called New Troy, under which name it continued a long time after . . .'

Lulled by the familiar words, I sat back and studied the audience. Tonight's ceremony was attended by the usual mix of politicians, B-list celebrities and minor royals. Most of the front rows were taken by the Trinovantum Council. It's an all-male organisation, which claims to originate with the knights King Brutus appointed to protect the temple. Their leader is the Lord Herne. His job is to witness and interpret the High

Priestess's oracles; the other members raise funds and campaign for the cult.

When it came to the ritual thanksgiving, I did my best to feel grateful for the council's good works. Still, looking out at all those well-fed faces and self-important smiles, I couldn't help feeling that our real supporters were the ones waiting outside in the damp and the dark.

It was soon time to join them. We lit our torches at the altar fire and marched outside to the beat of a drum, the clash of cymbals and a storm of camera flashes from the crowd. The solemnity of the ceremony gave way to something of a party atmosphere as everyone took their places for the parade.

The order of the procession hadn't changed for centuries. The first float always carries the image of the goddess, accompanied by Opis in her golden chariot and followed by the cult. Behind us was the Lord Herne, dressed as a huntsman with a green cloak and a crown of antlers on his head (in the Greek myths, Artemis's companion is Orion; Herne is his Celtic counterpart). Then came a man on horseback playing the part of King Brutus, a statue of the giant Gogmagoc and a marching band. Afterwards, we'd have fireworks and a roast venison dinner. I'd been looking forward to it for weeks. We all had.

Before we could set off, however, we had to get through the Lord Herne's speech. It seemed to go on for even longer than usual. Our torches sputtered and smoked, the firelight flickering eerily on Gogmagoc's crazed eyes. I stood among the other handmaidens and tried to hide my shivers.

The veils weren't much of a disguise if you knew the personalities under them. I could tell from the tilt of her head that Cally was looking down her nose. Twitchy Iphigenia kept fiddling with her sleeve. The little twins, Niobe and Chione, were standing as close together as possible. Arethusa's veil was fixed crooked and her hem was grubby. Phoebe's eyes kept sliding over to the boys in the crowd. At thirteen, she was the oldest after Cally and me, and I didn't reckon she'd make it as far as initiation.

The person Phoebe was eyeing the most was the man acting the part of Brutus. He was young, and looked uncannily like the depiction of the king in the temple mosaics: thick bronze hair, a square pale face, broad shoulders. He must have been recently elected to the Trinovantum Council, for I hadn't seen him before.

Phoebe adjusted her veil, accidently-on-purpose flashing a smile in his direction. Cally kicked her in the ankle with the stealth and efficiency born of long practice. I hoped people would think Phoebe's squeal was one of excitement at the Lord Herne's speech.

'In times of darkness,' he was saying, 'we look for the light of faith –'

'Shame!'

It took a few moments before people realised what was happening. There was a disturbance at the back of the crowd, and more shouting. 'For shame!' the voice bellowed again. 'Liars and frauds!' Tuts of disapproval turned into a babble of dismay.

A man wrestled his way towards the assembled dignitaries. He was tall and lean, with rolling dark eyes and a shock of curls. He carried a small wicker hamper in one hand, and pointed at the High Priestess with the other. 'The Holy One sees your crimes! You have silenced her voice! Stolen the oracle!'

I flinched at the words. This, surely, would undo all the good of our prayers and fasting. I wanted to cover my eyes and ears, to shut out the blasphemy before it could infect me too.

Then the man tipped the hamper over. A knot of black ropes spilled on to the ground in front of Opis. They hissed and writhed.

Not ropes . . . snakes. A seething, slithering tangle of shiny black serpents.

Several people started screaming. The twins began to cry. Those nearest the snakes pushed and shoved each other in a panicked effort to move back. I, however, was rooted to the spot. One of the serpents had reared its head and seemed to be looking straight at me, its eyes like two drops of shining black blood. Its forked tongue licked the air; my breath choked, as if the snake's coils were already tightening round my throat. *Artemis, save us . . .*

My prayer was answered. A resourceful councillor dragged over a plastic waste bin and threw it over the snakes. At the same time, the King Brutus impersonator jumped down from his horse and rugby-tackled the interloper to the ground. The man flailed about wildly, and managed to tear himself free, just for a moment. He flung himself towards Opis. I was nearest to her, and amid the shouting and panic and general confusion I was unsure whether anyone else heard him.

'I'm warning you, Bella,' he said. 'You can't go on –'

King Brutus slammed into him again and he came crashing down for a second time. Two policemen came to help and the man was dragged away, still ranting, with a bloodied nose. The crowd broke into applause.

I wanted to clap too. I felt a rush of pride in our High Priestess, so calm and so dignified.

But after the snakes were removed, the speeches finished, and we moved into line for the procession, I saw Brutus's gold laurel wreath lying discarded on the ground. There was blood on it, from where the man had been dragged away.

Though I didn't realise it at the time, it had been a night of omens. Sometimes the gods speak to us and we just don't recognise the signs.

CHAPTER 2

The morning after the festival was shopping day. Once a month, representatives from the smart department stores are ushered into the priestesses' sitting room to display their merchandise. There's cooing and squealing, the rustle of tissue paper, and a tropical-scented mist from the competing perfumes sprayed in the air.

'Girls, girls,' scolded one of the older priestesses, as Phoebe and Iphigenia squabbled over a pair of designer sunglasses. 'We are *pagans*, not savages. Only real ladies may serve the goddess.'

This was a bit of an exaggeration. Admittedly, it used to be a big deal to get accepted as a handmaiden. Deserving charity cases were occasionally taken in, but for the most part, only the crème de la crème could boast of having a priestess of Artemis in the family. These days, however, we were more of a mixed bag. Because Artemis is a virgin goddess, so are her attendants, and that kind of commitment didn't hold much appeal in the modern age.

It was true that Phoebe's parents were seriously posh and that Callisto's mother was once an It Girl. But Arethusa was left here by her father, one of the bankers embroiled in the banking collapse. Last we heard, he was living off his ill-gotten gains in Brazil. Iphigenia's dad is terminally ill; her mother asked the cult to take her in because she couldn't cope with looking after five children on her own. The twins were orphaned in the Brighton terror attacks.

I assumed there was a similar story in my own family's background. Bankruptcy, bereavement, breakdown. It was probably better not to know. Our pasts were wiped clean once we came here. We were given a new identity with our new names. The same names that Artemis's priestesses had always been given, taken from her mythology and passed down through the centuries. I was the latest Aura among the hundreds, perhaps thousands, who had gone before.

And it was the name thing that was bothering me. I was thinking about it even as I was trying to decide which shade of nail polish would go best with my new turquoise sandals.

The man with the snakes hadn't just called our High Priestess a liar and a fraud. He'd called her Bella. Her Christian name, not her pagan one. I'd heard her sister call her by it once, years ago, when she came to visit. Did that mean the madman knew Opis from her life before the cult?

Leto hobbled in as we were wrapping up our purchases. She was the oldest priestess here, wrinkled like a prune, with little wet blue eyes and a pinch as sly as Cally's. She didn't bother with shopping days, preferring an interchangeable selection of black velour tracksuits when she was off duty. 'You're wanted,' she told me in her sourest voice. 'Over in the palace.'

An impromptu chat with Opis wasn't an everyday occurrence. I saw Callisto look at me, eyes narrowed.

The two of us have more or less grown up together, and the older we got, the more our rivalry had sharpened. The reason was that in three or four years' time, Opis would retire. After she'd served her time, a High Priestess could leave the cult and would be given her own home and living allowance. Opis had had enough cosmetic procedures to look considerably younger than her real age, but after twenty years of service she'd be thinking about an election to find her successor.

The Trinovantum Council and the cult all had a vote and Cally, like me, had been sizing up the competition. Seven handmaidens, eight priestesses. The handmaidens below us would be too young; six of the priestesses were already too old. That left Atalanta, who was fat and a giggler, and Cynthia, who'd tried to run away twice, though each time she was back within a week.

So it was between the two of us. I was the quiet and reliable one, clever at my studies, dutiful at my chores. Cally, though, had charisma. She'd tell the little girls that they were stupid and ugly and deserved to be thrown out on the streets. Later, she would relent – allow them to brush her hair or share a cookie – and they'd be giddy with joy. As for the priestesses, the younger ones were charmed in spite of themselves; the older ones thought her flighty. Old Leto screwed up her face whenever she saw her. But Leto hated everyone.

The cult was all I had ever known. My home and my identity. My family, my career. That was why I wanted to become High Priestess. I wanted to tell the stories and lead the prayers. I wanted to know the workings of the oracle and to take my place on the Trinovantum Council's board. I wanted to retire, when I was forty or so, and have the choice of a new life . . .

Impressing the council and winning over the cult was important. But in the event of a tie Opis would cast the deciding vote. In any case, I was sure she could influence the outcome if she wanted to. That was why every meeting with her felt like an audition.

I nervously smoothed my clothes and set off across the wide lawn that separated our building, Artemisia House, from the High Priestess's Residence. It wasn't actually a palace, but a late-eighteenth-century town house of dark brown brick. The maid answered the bell. While she went to announce my arrival, I waited in the main reception room.

The room was lined with silver-grey silk and had little in the way of decoration. It didn't need it. As soon as you saw the painting on the wall it was hard to notice anything else. The Death of Actaeon, by Titian.

The story goes that the hunter Actaeon surprised the goddess bathing, and in revenge she turned him into a stag so that his hounds would kill him. Titian set the scene in an autumnal wood of golden leaves and dark storm clouds. The pursuing goddess is both stern and radiant, her flesh rounded, a copper burnish in her hair. Actaeon is caught in the moment of transformation from man to beast. His body twists backwards as his own dogs tear at his flesh.

'I never get tired of looking at it,' said Opis's voice behind me.

Startled, I turned round and touched my hand to my brow in greeting. 'Honoured Lady.'

Her eyes remained on the painting. 'It would be such a tragedy if we had to let it go.'

'Let it go?'

'Since the crash, our financial security cannot be guaranteed.' She gave an elegant shrug. 'Even a High Priestess needs to balance the books. But don't look so dismayed, Aura – we won't be selling the family silver just yet. I still have a few tricks up my sleeve.'

Opis's salon was in feminine contrast to the formality of the ground floor. The furniture was inlaid with mother-of-pearl and the pretty wallpaper featured birds of paradise. A host of framed photographs displayed Opis with the American ambassador, Opis with an uncomfortable-looking Archbishop of Canterbury, Opis at the royal wedding.

Her PA brought us tea and cinnamon biscuits as the Irish wolfhound, Argos, pressed its nose against my knee. The High Priestess always keeps a dog, but Opis had the look of a cat person, being slim and dark, with slanting eyes and high cheekbones, a precise red mouth. She sat back on the sofa and kicked off her heels with little purr of satisfaction.

'Did you enjoy the festival yesterday, Aura?'

'Very much, Honoured Lady.'

We made chit-chat about the weather, the guests, the Lord Herne's speech. Everything but the main talking point, in fact.

'The man with the snakes . . .' I began hesitantly.

Opis frowned. 'Lunatics are not worthy of our attention.'

'I know he must have been crazy. I just . . . I just wondered if you'd met him before, maybe? I mean, he knew your name. Your old one, that is.'

I regretted it at once. 'You are mistaken,' Opis said acidly. 'That is an absurd idea. Frankly, I find it a little disturbing that you are so determined to dwell on yesterday's unpleasantness. It suggests an appetite for drama and scandal that is unbecoming in a handmaiden of the cult.'

I lowered my head, ashamed. I sometimes worried that I had a knack for rubbing Opis up the wrong way. 'I'm very sorry, Honoured Lady. I didn't mean to cause offence.'

'Very well.' Opis granted me a gracious smile. 'We won't speak of it again. After all, there are much more important matters to attend to. The oracle warned us of tests to come.'

An oracle is always given at the festival, after the parade is over and the High Priestess and the Lord Herne enter the temple alone. The High Priestess then descends to the Chamber of the Oracle, inhales the smoke of laurel leaves and other secret herbs, and waits for divine inspiration to strike. The prophecy that Opis had given yesterday spoke of 'a time of trial and a new hope'.

'What do you think of this election business, for instance?' she asked.

I nearly choked on my tea. Then I realised that she was talking about the general election. We didn't follow politics very closely in the cult, but I knew that the prime minister, Nicholas Riley, had just won a new term in office despite the Electoral Commission finding evidence of vote-rigging and fraud.

'It's very troubling, Honoured Lady. The country lacks leadership.' I searched for something intelligent to say. 'However, maybe this could be a chance for the cult to take a more active role in public life?'

'Indeed it could. I worry, however, that some of us have become a little too set in our ways. A little too *complacent*.' She paused. 'However, I believe you, Aura, are different. It strikes me that you are a realist. Not a romantic.'

'I think priestesses need to be a bit of both.'

'Well, it's clear you're a credit to the cult. Your teachers speak very highly of you. I enjoyed reading the choral ode you composed in Greek class last week. "Star-jewelled queen of the midnight chase . . ."' She repeated it in Greek. 'Quite charming.'

'Thank you, Honoured Lady.'

'But learning is not everything, you know – leadership requires something more. Grace and poise can't be learned from books.'

I realised I was fidgeting with my teacup and, with effort, stilled my hands. 'No, Honoured Lady.'

'As it happens, I'm holding a supper party here tomorrow. Just a few Trinovantum guests and their friends. I'd like you to come.'

I was given little chance to express my thanks. Opis was already ringing for her assistant to show me out. As I was leaving, she licked a smudge of cinnamon off her finger, neat as a cat. 'Ask Callisto to pop round, will you?'

I had been a guest at quite a few society events. Horse racing at Ascot . . . rowing at Henley . . . opera at

Glyndebourne. On these occasions, cult representatives were mostly silent and decorative. A private dinner party was different. It was an honour to be asked, but it would also be a test of my social skills and networking ability. Cally's too, presumably.

I went back to Artemisia House and into the hand-maidens' sitting room to tell Cally that Opis wanted to see her as well. She and the rest of the girls were sprawled on the over-sized velvet sofas, watching a Disney film. The floor was littered with shopping bags and wrapping paper, as well as boxes of chocolates that had been left at the temple for us on Festival Day. Since our allowance was given in the form of credit marks rather than money, I didn't know much about the actual business of pounds and pence. Until Opis threatened to sell the Titian, I'd never really thought about how our shopping habit was paid for.

Artemisia House was by far the largest of the set of buildings, known as the Sanctuary, that occupies the block between the Temple of Artemis and Newgate Street. The house was rebuilt at the height of Victorian swagger and was far too big for us.

A grand staircase of treacle-dark wood led to a warren of shadowy corridors and cavernous rooms. In spite of their size, they always looked cluttered, thanks to an abundance of antiques (gifted to the cult by wealthy patrons) and temple bric-a-brac. Embroidered altar cloths and tapestries lined the walls; the alcoves were filled with statues of classical heroes and decorative bronze urns. And then there were the stuffed animals, which lined the halls in glass cases like a zoo for the dead. Wolves, boar, even a leopard . . . eyes glassy, fangs bared.

As I climbed the stairs to our dormitory, I started to wonder about the cost of heating and lighting the building, not to mention the army of domestic staff employed to look after it. It was time I got some financial know-how, I decided. Surely it was a good sign that Opis had told me it was a requirement of her job.

I felt a fizz of anticipation. Things were changing and I had a part to play. 'I'm going to a party,' I said aloud, as I stood in the empty dormitory.

Then I thought how the evening would be full of stern old men and pompous dowagers. Everyone there would be assessing my table manners and conversation, comparing my charm to Callisto's. My high spirits evaporated.

I pulled off my headscarf. It was white silk, and worn draped over the hair and round the neck. When we were required to veil up, we drew one end across the lower face and pinned it to the other side. But I'd expected to be bare-faced at a private dinner party. Among strangers, it would feel like nakedness.

I looked in the mirror and practised my smile. My face stared back, unconvinced.

Cally's cheeks had the same rosy flush, her hair the same coppery-gold gleam, as the goddess in Titian's paint-ing. Her blue eyes glowed with holiness. Mine were washed-out grey. I was small and skinny. My hair was fine and dusty-fair, my skin pale as a ghost's. Next to Cally, I was colourless.

I didn't start off colourless. I was famous, in fact: the baby left on the temple's steps as a gift for Artemis. There were only two handmaidens when I arrived, and they graduated to priestesses a couple of years later. In the beginning I was everyone's pet, the cult's lucky charm. But as I grew older my novelty wore off. Sometimes I was a nuisance, mostly I was a non-entity. I was always alone.

So I prayed to Artemis to send me a friend. I got Callisto instead.

According to gossip I overheard from the cleaners, Callisto's mother was on the edge of celebrity, thanks to a bit of acting and some famous boyfriends – though which of these was responsible for Cally has never been clear. Following a stint in rehab, she'd gone public about putting her daughter in the temple to 'give her a better life'.

Intrigued and excited, I watched the new handmaiden's arrival from an archive store that overlooked Temple Square. I wasn't the only one: word had spread, and a crowd had gathered.

Paparazzi sprang into action when a car swept into the square and a dainty little girl in a pink frock got out. She was followed by a woman in a very tight dress and dark glasses. Cameras whirred and clicked as the pair climbed the temple steps to where Opis was waiting to receive them. Mother and daughter embraced, the woman removing her glasses to brush away a single glistening tear. The girl turned to wave goodbye to the crowd. She was perfectly posed, perfectly adorable.

Her own tears came later. A whole tantrum's worth of them, according to the whispers in the priestesses' sitting room. When she finally came into the room we were to share, I saw that even red eyes and crying-blotches couldn't obscure her prettiness.

'Hello,' I said. 'I'm Aura.'

She regarded me silently. Then she reached over and

gave my hair a yank, so hard I yelped. Tears of shock sprang into my eyes.

'Ow! Why'd you do that?'

Callisto smiled. It was a smile I'd get to know very well over the years: satisfied, secretive, shining with righteousness.

'Because the goddess told me to.'

The goddess told Callisto many things. On any given day, she might instruct her to take the last slice of cake, to blame me for a stained altar cloth or trip up the younger girls when they were noisy in the corridor. Whereas I'd been dumped on the temple steps like any old rubbish, she, Callisto, had been Chosen. Artemis had appeared to her in a dream and called her to the cult.

Her mother still visited, occasionally. Sometimes she was polished to a high-impact shine; sometimes she was dishevelled and her eyes didn't focus properly. In the first year after Cally joined us, her mother made regular appearances in the press, gushing about her daughter, 'Artemis's Own Angel', and the heart-rending sacrifice of giving her up.

The cult wasn't above a bit of PR spin either. Last year, there was a special feature in the *Daily Mail*, complete with a soft-focus shot of Cally in ceremonial robes, gazing pensively out of a window. According to the journalist, our days were a merry round of 'sacred rituals, charitable works and feminine accomplishments'. Cally and I, of course, had turned all these things into a competition.

The day of the dinner party, Opis decreed that Cally and I were to move out of the dormitory into a double room. The peace and quiet would help us prepare for our initiations next week. And so we'd been put back in the room we'd shared when Cally first joined the cult. Nothing had changed, from the two four-poster beds with tasselled canopies to the wardrobe the size of a small bathroom. It had been one of Cally's favourite games to lock me in it before prayers.

Once we'd unpacked, it was time to get ready for the evening. I fingered last month's shopping-day purchase: a pale green chiffon dress with a beaded bodice. But only priestesses got to wear their own clothes to private social functions; the rest of us used any excuse to get dressed up – Phoebe had even been known to wear a ballgown to Sunday lunch. I turned away from the chiffon and reached for a clean navy tunic and my special-occasion mantle with a border of embroidered peacock feathers.

'Feeling nervous?' Cally asked, smoothing down her veil.

'No. Why do you say that?'

'You're doing that weird thing with your lower lip. Pulling it out. You always do it when you're anxious. It's kind of disgusting.'

I abruptly moved my hand from my mouth. Callisto, as ever, knew me far too well.

'Poor Aura. I know how awkward you get on social occasions. Follow my lead, and you'll be fine.' Her voice was sugar with a dose of syrup. 'You might as well start getting used to it.'

CHAPTER 3

There were two reception rooms in the High Priestess's Residence. The Silver Room housed the Titian, and the Gold adjoined the dining room at the back of the house. Cally and I entered the Gold Room together, side by side.

Opis had arranged for us to arrive last so that our entrance would have maximum impact. She glided over to greet us, wearing a low-cut black evening gown and the pearl headdress she used for parties. 'How lovely to see you, my dears.' She gave a conspiratorial smile. 'Why don't you show yourselves to our friends?'

Cally and I drew back our veils. It would be the first time members of the Trinovantum Council had seen our faces. Opis knew what she was doing – a dash of theatricality is part of what's kept the cult going over the years.

Silence fell. *Eyes front, shoulders back*, I told myself. *Don't let them see you flinch.*

Before the moment could go on too long, Opis drew us into the room and started making introductions. The most prominent guest was Lionel Winter, the head of the Trinovantum Council and the Lord Herne. He was a frequent visitor to the Sanctuary and was a handsome man, thin-lipped, with a high domed forehead and a sweep of silvery-blond hair. He was accompanying the Honoured Apollonia, who had been High Priestess before Opis. A doll-like woman in her mid sixties, she blinked at the gathering with faded blue eyes as if she couldn't quite work out what she was doing there. Since her retirement she rarely visited the cult, and she seemed keen to keep her visit that evening to a minimum, slipping away soon after Cally and I arrived.

Of the other guests, I already knew the hawk-faced Lady Sudely, one of our major donors, and the shrivelled old council treasurer and his even more shrivelled wife. The two younger councillors with whom they were standing were the type Cally called chinless wonders, and who always pop up at this kind of event.

Gathered together, these people were even more than usually intimidating. Without the veil to hide my emotions, I could feel my face turning as wooden as a doll's.

'Let me introduce you to my nephew, Sebastian,' said Winter as a tall young man turned from the fireplace.

It was King Brutus. He shook my and Cally's hands, looking just as regal and bored as when he was riding in the parade. 'Call me Seb.'

'And I'm Scarlet,' announced the girl next to him. She had a dishevelled crop of dark hair and glossy lips the same colour as her name. I could see Cally eyeing her dress disapprovingly. It was leopard print, skimpy yet expensive-looking, accessorised by towering black stilettos. She certainly wasn't the usual kind of visitor to the cult. She must be the daughter of some big patron, I decided.

Small talk was mostly confined to the festival and, as others joined us, the shocking episode with the snakes. Various people lamented the scandalous state of social services that meant that hordes of lunatics were free to wander the streets. Seb's bravery in tackling the man was widely praised.

'You must have been right at the centre of things,' one of the chinless wonders said to me. 'Any clues as to what the nutter was on about?'

I was pretty sure he was joking, but I could feel Opis's eyes on me. 'Uh, no. Not at all. I was just too, you know, shocked.'

'Poor Aura's always been highly strung,' Cally said. She turned to me, a look of tender concern on her face. 'I really thought you were going to pass out with fright.'

Before I could think of any sort of comeback, the conversation had moved on.

My best hope was that the attention would go to Cally's head. She'd already had quite a lot of champagne. Maybe she'd become flighty, indiscreet. While Opis was distracted by Lady Sudely, I took the opportunity to slip out into the hall. I needed a moment to collect myself.

Click-clack-click went the tap of toenails on polished wood. 'Argos!' I whispered. 'What are you doing here?' The wolfhound looked at me with mournful eyes. His tail wagged in apology.

Opis wouldn't want him on the loose. As I looked around for the maid, Argos trotted off, nudging open the door to the Silver Room across the way. Muttering under my breath, I went to retrieve him.

Argos wasn't alone. A stranger was standing in front of the Titian. He was unlikely to be a burglar, since he was dressed for dinner in white tie and tails. I tried to grab Argos's collar and back away before we were spotted, but the dog wriggled free.

The unknown guest, however, barely glanced in our

direction. His eyes were fixed on the painting as he began to speak.

> 'For beauty is nothing
> but the beginning of terror, which we still are just
>   able to endure,
> and we are so awed by because it serenely disdains
> to annihilate us . . .'

For the second time in two days I stared at Actaeon's agony, the goddess's vengeful gleam. The words hummed through my body, almost as if I'd heard them before. The guest had recited the verse quite softly and unselfconsciously, as if he was talking to himself.

'Sorry,' he said abruptly, turning round. I saw he was younger than I'd thought at first, only a couple of years older than me. 'I'm not usually so pretentious at parties. I'm Aiden. Which one are you?'

As if we were all interchangeable. I put a hand on Argos's wiry grey head for reassurance. 'I'm Aura. It's nice to meet you.' He might be rude, but I couldn't afford to make a bad impression.

I'm used to being gawped at; it goes with the uniform. But of course a handmaiden unveiled is even more of a spectacle. Now that this Aiden person was giving me his full attention, he made no attempt to hide his curiosity. His look was bold, assessing, amused. I felt myself flush, though I didn't lower my eyes.

His own appearance didn't have much to recommend it. The suit was too small for his rangy frame and he'd pushed the sleeves back over his wrists. The cuffs didn't look particularly clean, and nor did his thatch of shaggy hair. The face under it was thin and brown, with alert green eyes.

'What was the poem you quoted?' I asked.

'It's by Rilke. From the *Duino Elegies* . . . But I suppose you only know Greek and Latin stuff.'

'Does that make me even more pretentious than you?'

Although he laughed, he looked slightly taken aback. He turned to study the painting again.

'Makes you wonder why Artemis is still so popular. You have to admit she's an almighty bitch.'

'Maybe the fact that she's flawed is part of her appeal.' I was angry, but wasn't going to give him any satisfaction by showing it. 'The ancient Greek gods really were just like us. They made mistakes, held grudges, had favourites. Artemis is an immortal who understands what it's like to be human.'

Aiden raised his eyebrows. 'While her cult is an organisation that understands what it's like to be divine. Praised, protected, showered with presents. And no questions asked.'

I'd never heard anyone speak about us in this way. I looked at him again, trying to work out what kind of person would say such things. I saw now that perhaps he was handsome, in an unkempt sort of way. The realisation unsettled me.

I lifted my chin. 'Is that why you've come to dinner – you think we owe you some presents?'

'You're funny.'

'And you're patronising.' As soon as I said it, I regretted my rudeness. What had got into me?

But our guest didn't seem offended. In fact, he gave me a comical little bow. 'My apologies. And please don't tell Opis. She's even scarier than Artemis, I hear.'

'Um, perhaps we should join the other guests,' I suggested, after an awkward pause.

'Oh God – Goddess, I mean.' He tugged at his collar. 'I was hoping to hide out here. In all honesty, I'd almost prefer to be ripped apart by that hound of yours.'

Argos wagged his tail obligingly.

I let the new arrival go ahead into the Gold Room, and managed to deliver the dog to the housekeeper before returning to the party. Luckily, Opis's attention was elsewhere. She was talking to Lionel Winter, who had an arm round Aiden's shoulder. Was Aiden another nephew, perhaps? I'd thought him self-assured – annoyingly so. But here he looked hunched and sullen. His face only lightened when Scarlet came up to him and kissed him on the cheek. Afterwards, they went to giggle in a corner like naughty children. I felt an unwelcome twinge of envy. What would it be like to have another person with whom to share a joke or hide away at a party?

At long last, we made our way into the dining room. The mahogany banqueting table was laden with china and candles and flowers. Candlelight glinted off the silver, sparked off the glass. I found I would be sitting next to Lionel Winter, with one of the chinless wonders on my other side.

Cally was a little way down the table, between the Trinovantum treasurer and Seb Winter. She was bright-eyed and pink-cheeked, and tendrils of hair escaped from her headscarf. Even so, I'd done better on the seating. To be placed next to the Lord Herne was an honour.

'Tell me, Aura, why do you think the cult remains popular in an otherwise secular age?' he asked as the fish course was brought in.

I paused, aware that others on the table were preparing to listen, and tried to block out Aiden's mocking grin. 'We're not like other religions,' I said. 'Nobody's bribed with the idea of heaven, or threatened with hell. We offer reassurance for the here and now.'

The people around me nodded and smiled. But Aiden gave a loud snort.

'You offer reassurance to those who can afford it, and mumbo-jumbo to all the rest.'

Everyone looked down at their plates, embarrassed, except for Scarlet, who laughed. It was like the blasphemy of the man with the snakes, only worse, because Aiden was sane.

However, our High Priestess didn't so much as blink. 'I'm sorry you see the mystery of the oracle as "mumbo-jumbo". When Artemis favours me with a prophecy, I feel her truth shine through me like a great light.'

'That's good to hear, but I'd have thought a god invading your mind would be a little more disruptive. Violent, in fact.' Aiden popped some bread in his mouth and chomped noisily. 'Because that's what the oracle is meant to be, isn't it – a kind of demonic possession?'

'You're thinking of the old stories, in which our goddess is something of a femme fatale.' Opis spoke with admirable restraint. 'These days, we take a more metaphorical view of her mythology.'

'Wasn't she always blasting people with thunderbolts?' asked Scarlet.

'A bow and arrow,' said Seb. 'Or else she was turning them into animals. Like your namesake.' He nodded at Cally, who smiled and blushed, though she generally dislikes being reminded of the original Callisto's downfall. Being turned into a bear isn't very dignified.

'I don't think those stories are so important,' I said hesitantly. 'The myth that people really want to believe is the one of Artemis leading Brutus to his new kingdom. Because there is always a war, we hope there will always be a survivor. Following a vision in search of better things.'

'I'll drink to that,' said Aiden. 'And to the goddess continuing to protect her own. Cheers!' He raised his glass. 'Here's to staying nice and cosy in the Sanctuary.' He smiled brightly round the table. 'Fiddling while London burns.'

'Why did you disappear halfway through drinks?' Cally demanded, almost as soon as the door to our room shut behind us.

'It was stuffy. I needed some air.'

'You were skulking around with that awful Aiden boy.'

'Hardly. I bumped into him in the hall.'

I didn't want to think, let alone talk, about Aiden. Everything about him was unsettling.

'Well, he's a delinquent,' Cally announced. 'Seb told me. They used to go to the same school. Aiden was only invited tonight because his father is in business with Lionel Winter, and Lionel owed him a favour.'

Seb had been watching Cally that evening, from under heavy-lidded eyes. So had all the men, at one time or other. The more jovial they became, the more demure Cally became. Perhaps sexy King Brutus was part of the test, along with the champagne. His Uncle Lionel was no doubt preparing him for a leading role within the council. And a new High Priestess gets a new Lord Herne . . . Maybe I shouldn't have been so pleased with the seating plan after all.

As I lay in the darkness, I forced myself to confront what life would be like if Cally was High Priestess. If I had to call her Honoured Lady. Arrange flowers for her dinner parties. Polish her headdresses.

A law was passed in 1979 to decriminalise priestesses who abandoned the cult. However, outsiders could still be prosecuted for encouraging or assisting a priestess to leave and, without back-up, most runaways didn't last very long. It might have been possible five or six years ago, but with the country on the brink of all sorts of disasters it would be the worst of times to start a new life. I would have no money, no qualifications, no connections. No practical knowledge of the outside world.

In the sleepless hours that followed, I could hear Cally tossing and turning on the other side of the room. I tried to remind myself that it was a good sign that she was worried too.

CHAPTER 4

'Aiden's a delinquent,' said Opis over coffee the next day. 'Though a minor one. He comes from a very good family indeed. *Such* a pity.'

She told me he was the son of the banker Philip Carlyle, one of the Trinovantum Council's most distinguished members, and a close business associate of Lionel Winter. Mr Carlyle was now retired and lived in the Cayman Islands with his wife. It was hoped and expected that Aiden would take his place in the council, now that he'd turned eighteen. The family had always been very generous supporters of the cult.

But Aiden showed no appreciation for the privileges and opportunities given to him. First he got kicked out of his fancy boarding school, then he took part in an anti-government demonstration that turned into a riot. He'd been arrested and charged with public order offences, and sentenced to community service.

'He can be a little challenging, as we saw at dinner,' Opis said, stirring her coffee with a silver spoon. 'But I think this rebelliousness is merely a phase. I don't believe it runs deep.'

I could see that hard-core delinquents didn't usually quote German lyric poetry. But I didn't understand why I'd been summoned to a private meeting with Opis just to chat about Aiden Carlyle. I kept expecting to be reprimanded for something. Then Opis explained that Mr Carlyle had phoned his old chum Lionel Winter, to ask if Aiden's community service could be carried out at the cult.

'We thought he could be of use in the archive,' Opis said blandly. 'Do some filing and so forth. Since archive work is one of your specialities, I was hoping you would increase your hours there to help supervise.'

I opened my mouth and then closed it.

'Leto will, of course, be on hand to manage and chaperone.'

My heart sank some more. Leto is Head Archivist. She would resent the intrusion and would no doubt take it out on me.

'With a bit of luck, this spot of bother with the law shouldn't harm Aiden's long-term prospects. Considering his family's wealth and connections, he could be a real asset to this cult. We need to make him feel welcome, and keep him engaged.'

So we were going to overlook Aiden's blasphemy? His complete disrespect for everything we stood for? I decided that there must be further extenuating circumstances that the High Priestess was unable to share with me. The only thing I felt certain of was that I really, really didn't want to have to deal with Aiden again.

'I understand, Honoured Lady.'

'*Perfect.* I know I can count on you.'

The cult's archive is housed in a building overlooking Temple Square, the other side from the Sanctuary. The display room is open to the public by appointment. There you can see the famous oracles of ages past, like the ones that predicted the Gunpowder Plot and the death of Nelson, written down by the Lord Hernes of the time on vellum bound with silk.

Many of the records I looked after went back centuries. They included lists of donations, the Sanctuary's visitors' books, menus from festival feasts, shopping lists and accounts. I usually worked in the main office for two afternoons a week, sorting and cataloguing.

The archive was Leto's lair. She spent most of her time there drinking black coffee and reading out-of-date magazines in a back room. I quite liked being left alone with the paperwork. It helped that Cally avoided archive duty where at all possible. Up until now, the place had been a refuge.

Aiden turned up at the agreed time looking even scruffier than he had at the dinner, unshaven and with red-rimmed eyes. Leto and I were both veiled and he peered at us dubiously when we met him at the door.

'You're the one from the party?' he asked me.

'Yes. Aura. It's . . . er . . . nice to see you again.'

'Where's your mutt?'

'It's not mine. It belongs to the High Priestess.'

'Oh. I thought it was part of the security settings. To guard your virtue.'

'That's my job,' said Leto with a sniff. 'Though to be honest, young man, you don't have the brawn to be a threat or the looks to be a temptation.'

I blushed beneath my veil. Aiden, however, seemed to find this hilarious.

'Fair point. OK, ladies – show me to the spreadsheets.'

*　　*　　*

44

Aiden's community service was going to be spent entering data into the new online database. It had recently been set up for everyone who had consulted the oracle over the last hundred years, and we needed to input the pre-digital records.

'Oof,' he said, putting his head in his hands as the computer hummed into life. 'The morning after the night before.'

He turned round and looked at Leto beseechingly. 'I don't suppose you could spare this hopeless delinquent a drop of coffee?'

To my surprise, she brought him a cup from her ancient coffee maker. I've never been offered any, or dared to ask.

Aiden took a gulp and winced. 'Goddess. That'll put hair on your chest.' When Leto had returned, muttering, to her sofa, he pushed the cup towards me. 'Want some?'

'No, thank you.'

'C'mon, live a little. Don't tell me that artificial stimulants are against the rules – we all know the oracle's one big chemical high.'

I kept my eyes on my papers. 'I'd just rather not risk the chest hair.'

To my relief, he settled down after this and worked quietly for the next couple of hours. I could feel his eye on me now and again. But he didn't try to make conversation. Leto 'supervised' from the comfort of her beaten-up sofa in the room next door.

Towards the end of the afternoon, Opis dropped by to check on our progress. 'Dear Aura is so meticulous,' she said to Aiden, with a benevolent smile. 'She has a natural talent for this sort of work.'

I wondered if this was the future she saw for me. The next Head Archivist, the next Leto. Shut up among the dust and ink while Cally swanned about in a moonstone headdress . . . I'd go insane.

After the High Priestess had gone, Aiden paused by my desk on his way back from the storeroom. I was transcribing a list of donations made to the cult in 1981.

He bent to take a look over my shoulder and whistled.

'Nice. Just as well you ladies don't have to take a vow of poverty.'

'I should have realised you don't believe in paying for things,' I said, moving my seat from under his shadow. 'You go looting instead.'

'Hey – I wasn't looting. Or rioting, for that matter. I was part of a peaceful protest against the government's alliance with corrupt capitalists. Things only got out of hand when the police started charging us with batons.'

Leto seemed to have nodded off over her pile of mouldering *Good Housekeeping* magazines. I lowered my voice. 'Corrupt capitalists? Isn't your father a banker?'

'Yep.' His face darkened. 'And he's as crooked as they come. A greedy bully, just like the rest.'

'Well, having a crook in the family obviously has some advantages.' I tried to keep my tone neutral. 'That's why you're drinking coffee here, instead of picking up litter or scrubbing stairwells in some tower-block estate.'

'Fair point. However, I didn't do anything wrong and so I don't believe I should be punished.' He leaned back in his chair and regarded me narrowly. 'I mean, d'you actually know how bad things are? Out in the real world?'

'I'm not an idiot.'

'I never said you were. But you do lead a very sheltered life. So, for instance, are you aware that the unemployment rate is now at one in three? Or that over the last five years suicides have rocketed by thirty per cent, homelessness by twenty-five? There've been riots outside food banks in Birmingham and Bristol, anarchist bombs in the City. Drug gangs are fighting running battles in the middle of London . . .'

I'd always been told that a priestess's conversation should demonstrate that she is both educated and well-informed. Which was easier said than done, seeing as our schooling was almost exclusively Classical Studies; we weren't allowed to access the internet and our newspapers were censored. Aiden might have a point. Even so, I resented his patronising tone.

'Shouting slogans and waving banners is hardly going to fix anything.'

'Demanding free and fair elections might,' he retorted. 'And it sure as hell beats praying for divine intervention . . . Seriously, Aura, doesn't it bother you that the country's on the brink of collapse and yet it's business as usual for the temple and Trinovantum gang?'

'Of course it upsets me.' In fact, I was embarrassed. I'd had no idea things were so bad. 'And you're right: the cult ought to be doing more for charity.'

'The cult's only interested in feathering its own nest.'

'That's not true.'

All the same, I felt a twinge of doubt. When Opis had lamented the state of our finances, there hadn't been any mention of providing for the poor. It was all about keeping cult treasures like the Titian painting intact. To reassure myself as much as Aiden, I said, 'We wouldn't be so popular if people thought we were greedy and uncaring.'

'True,' he said thoughtfully, as if to himself. 'If

anything, you're gaining in popularity. Just as people are losing faith in everything else this country stands for . . . And popularity means power. I wonder what Opis and Lionel will do with it?'

It was a relief when Aiden left. I didn't like to think that we were deliberately kept in ignorance about events outside the Sanctuary walls. Aiden's remarks about the cult's power made me uncomfortable too. I remembered how easily Opis had dismissed my question about the man with the snakes, and how meekly I'd accepted it.

Scarlet, the girl who'd come to the dinner party, was waiting for Aiden to finish his shift. I peeped out of the archive window to get a better view of her outfit: black leather leggings and low-cut metallic top. According to Cally, she was a slut. According to the porter, she was the daughter of the rock star Rick Moodie. His last album had been named *Artemis Unchained*, and he was trying to get Opis to give him a private oracle.

I watched Scarlet sling her arm round Aiden's shoulders and say something that made him laugh. I felt a pang. Not for the romance, I told myself, but the companionship. The Greek myths depict love as a bloodstained and vengeful business, and my only other source of information on the subject was the gossip mags that careless staff sometimes left in the bins. The stories in those are pretty vengeful too, full of jealousy and drama and betrayal.

But Scarlet and Aiden's relationship didn't look full of drama. They just looked like they were having fun.

Aiden and Scarlet weren't the only dinner-party guests to revisit the Sanctuary soon afterwards. A few days later, on my way across the lawn, I heard voices in the High Priestess's garden. I glanced through the wrought-iron gate to see Seb Winter and Cally strolling on the lawn. Cally wasn't veiled. Her head was lowered modestly, but she was gesturing animatedly as she talked. Seb didn't seem to be saying much. Even in the sunshine, his pale, regular features had a chilly sort of look, as if carved from marble.

'How's King Brutus?' I asked her after dinner, my curiosity getting the better of me.

'King –? Oh . . . you mean Seb.' Her smile was sleek. 'He's well. He's writing a magazine article about the younger generation of Trinovantum Councillors and their relations with the cult. Opis has asked me to help him with our side of the story.'

I thought of Brutus's square jaw and heavy brow, and how Cally's face had glowed in the sunshine. But Cally was surely too smart to allow herself to be compromised. She must know what she was doing. So must Opis.

Still, I was curious about Seb and his role within the council. The next day, I even asked Aiden about him, trying a casual, roundabout approach.

'Your family must be disappointed you're not joining the Trinovantum.'

'Not really. They think I'd only do it to cause trouble. Which is tempting, I'll admit.'

'Sebastian Winter is quite active on the board. I . . . I heard you went to school together.'

'So?'

'I just wondered how well you knew him.'

Aiden raised one eyebrow. 'I know he's a thug. A thug and a bore who's being groomed for greatness by his uncle Lionel. Why d'you ask?'

I glanced over in Leto's direction. Our chaperone was cackling over the problem pages of *Women's Own*.

'No reason. He's just been hanging around the Sanctuary a lot.'

'Hmm.' He tipped back in his chair. 'Setting hearts aflutter, no doubt. I'd be careful if I were you. Seb Winter takes no prisoners.'

I regretted raising the subject. Starting any sort of

conversation with Aiden only gave him the chance to goad me. I resolved to maintain a dignified silence from here on. Unfortunately, that same afternoon Leto told me to give our 'volunteer' a tour of the oracle display room.

'You ever think about swapping the archive for the oracle?' he asked, as I showed him in.

'It's not up to me. The goddess calls her own.'

Aiden laughed. 'Yeah, right. I've heard that High Priestess elections are a cut-throat business. I doubt you'd be two-faced enough for the job – which is kind of a shame. You even look the part.'

'I do?' I was so surprised I spoke before realising it.

'It's your eyes. And your hair – all pale and silvery. A good match for a moonshine goddess.'

I didn't know what to say. I'd never thought of myself like that. As if I wasn't grey and shadowy but . . . silver.

Aiden's attention had already moved on to the display cases. 'Clever – like horoscopes,' was his verdict. 'You recycle enough vague phrases enough times, one or other of them will turn out to be relevant to something or somebody, somewhere.'

I pursed my lips. 'These predictions aren't vague. They're specific. Like the oracle about the Gunpowder Plot. It actually said where to find the plotters.'

'That'll be because somebody had already given the High Priestess a tip-off. The cult's always had its spies, and so has the council. I bet old Lionel's pillow talk is very informative.'

'What do you mean?'

'C'mon, surely you can't be that naive.' He was amused and – even more infuriating – pitying. 'Everyone knows he and your Honoured Lady are more than just good friends.'

'Don't be disgusting.'

I turned on my heel and went to the door. He put his hand on it to stop me leaving. His hand was like the rest of him – long and lean and brown. I stared at his bitten-down fingernails, my body tensed all over, ready to fight. But when he spoke his voice was gentle.

'You may be sheltered, Aura, but you're not immune to the real world. If you're going to make it in this place, you're going to need to be pretty hard-nosed. Else people will take advantage.'

I was glad he couldn't see my face. 'I don't take life lessons from smutty gossip.' I was only just able to keep my voice steady as I pushed past. 'Don't pretend you know anything about me or this cult.'

Later, though, I began to wonder. Aiden's family were Trinovantum insiders. That's why Opis wanted him, and his money, on-board. He could be as much of an insider as Seb, if he wanted.

Maybe he already was. Maybe all this heretical talk was designed to trip me up, entrap me . . . I remembered the feel of his hand on mine, and went hot and cold all over.

CHAPTER 5

'How is young Mr Carlyle doing?'

'He gets the work done, Honoured Lady. But he doesn't respect it, or us. He's too full of himself.'

'Adolescent posturing, no doubt. Young men can be slow to mature.'

'And learn manners, apparently.'

'Aura. You have started to become rather sharp. It's not an attractive quality.'

'I'm sorry, Honoured Lady.'

I passed Lionel Winter on my way out of the Residence. He greeted me with his usual distant courtesy, and I was ashamed to think of Aiden's insinuations.

Later that morning, I went to fetch a book and found Cally in our room. She was standing by the window, which overlooked the tall stone arch at the Sanctuary entrance. Seb and his uncle were talking with a man in military uniform by the gate. Her expression was unguarded and softer – younger – than I'd seen for a while. She didn't even hear me come and stand behind her until I said her name.

She started. 'Don't creep up on me like that!'

I sat on the bed.

'You know we have to be careful, right? About getting too involved with people outside the cult, I mean. Especially boys.'

'What are you implying?'

'Nothing bad.' I was thinking of Aiden as well as Seb. I didn't really believe he was trying to trap me and felt a little guilty about complaining about him to Opis. The trouble was I'd never met anyone who had such a knack for getting under my skin. Apart from Cally, of course. 'Just . . . well, it's easy to get a bit carried away.'

'Easy for you, perhaps. My reputation is impeccable and I intend to keep it that way. If you've disgraced yourself, then Artemis will be your judge. Opis too, of course, once she finds out.'

I knew how reckless I was being. But, just once, I wanted us to speak openly to each other.

'Cally . . . have you ever had any doubts that we're doing the right thing?'

'Doing what?'

'Becoming priestesses.'

Cally looked at me, and then towards the window. She bit her lip and got ready to speak. Then something in her tightened.

'Of course not. Unlike you, I have a calling. I've made my own choices the whole way, guided by the goddess.'

I felt a spurt of anger.

'Oh please. You were dumped here, same as me, because your mother wanted to keep on partying.'

Cally's eyes narrowed to slits. 'You have no faith. No sense of respect. No reverence. That's why you'll be calling me Honoured Lady in a couple of years' time.'

'Cally –'

'It's Callisto. Priestesses don't have nicknames.'

The next afternoon, Leto and I had an appointment at the British Library with a paper conservator who was helping carry out repairs on some of the archive material. Neither of us set off with any enthusiasm. 'I'm too old for this babysitting nonsense,' Leto harrumphed. 'Between you and that looter idiot, I get no peace.'

I didn't like leaving the Sanctuary at the best of times. Today was dark and wet and I had a headache. I was still feeling depressed about my conversation with Cally – Callisto – and the drive through the pouring rain did nothing to lift my spirits. Even in formerly affluent areas there was graffiti on the walls and piles of uncollected rubbish clogging the pavements. The people hurrying to get out of the rain had a hunched, anxious sort of look. I sat back in the warmth of our chauffeur-driven Daimler and was ashamed. Aiden was right: I'd been too sheltered for too long. It was time for me, and the cult, to go out into the real world and get our hands dirty.

Our business was done by five. No car, however, was waiting to collect us. A woman in the library's back office let us use her phone to call the Sanctuary. We were told our driver had got stuck behind a protest march in central London, so we should get a taxi and come home the long way round.

Aiden had said he was going on the march. He'd even suggested I should come along too. 'It would do you good to shout about something,' he'd said, waggling his eyebrows at me. 'I can see you're secretly dying to unleash your inner hooligan.'

I'd ignored him, of course. But shutting him out was getting harder. In fact, I couldn't stop thinking about our conversations. I just wished I could tell when he was annoyed with me, and when he was teasing.

The taxi firms we tried said it would be over an hour's wait. It took forty-five minutes standing in the rain before I managed to hail one. The driver was from Nigeria and thought we were nuns. At least he trusted us for the fare; priestesses don't carry cash or even mobile phones. Our uniform is supposed to be both passport and protection.

As we rattled through the city, the driver kept up a stream of grumbles. Petrol prices meant that hardly anyone could afford taxis and nobody tipped any more. The country was bust, and run by criminals. He should get out and go home. In the background, the radio warned of more chaos. Today's march was in response to the death of a political activist in police custody and had sparked 'disturbances' throughout the city –

We turned a corner and drove straight into the middle of one.

The dilapidated high street was jammed with cars and buses, some drivers honking and shouting, others abandoning their vehicles and heading for cover. A makeshift barricade had been set up at the end of the road from wedged-together cars. One had been overturned and set alight. A group of young men in hooded tops and red bandannas were standing in front of the barricade, armed with metal pipes. Another group in purple scarves advanced upon them, throwing bricks and stones. Then we heard gunshots.

The taxi driver was swearing and sweating but couldn't reverse because there were already more cars behind us. A young kid ran up, his face twisted with glee, and smashed a bat on the windscreen of the car.

'Out,' Leto wheezed, poking me with bony fingers. 'Out! Out!'

We scrambled from the backseat and fled into one of the side streets, joining a stream of other refugees. Our taxi driver wasn't far behind. It was every man for himself as people jostled to get away from the gunfire and the rising clouds of black smoke. I felt old and shaky, as feeble as Leto, my flimsy sandals pattering along on the pavement, my breath wheezing through the veil. *Artemis. Goddess. Protect your servants. Hear my prayer –*

'Aura?' said a disbelieving voice.

'Aiden!'

'Are you all right?'

I would never have guessed I could be so glad to see

him. 'I – we were on an errand, but nobody came to collect us, and then – then –' It was a struggle to get my voice under control. 'I don't know where we are, or what we should do –'

'It's OK. Let's get you out of here.'

He took me by one arm and Leto by another. I despised my own weakness, the sickly thumping of my heart that made me hold on to our escort like a frightened child.

Aiden was among a group of people who had come from the march. Some of them had bloody scrapes and torn clothing; the radio report had spoken of clashes with the police. But this was a different kind of conflict. As sirens sounded in the distance, there were screams as well as shots. A gaggle of young men on rusty motorbikes roared past us, heading into the fray.

'Who are these louts?' Leto panted.

'The guys in the red bandannas are the Hatchill Boyz,' Aiden said. 'The ones in purple are the Manor Town Crew. They started off as drugs gangs – now they're self-styled militia.' He looked round. 'Look, let's wait in here. I'll phone for back-up and we can stay put till things calm down a bit.'

He was pointing at a derelict shopping centre. The metal grille over the main entrance had been wrenched open and broken glass was scattered on the pavement.

Inside, it smelled sour and the only light came through the gaps in boarded-up windows. From what I could see, the shops had never been up to much. A plastic palm tree leaned drunkenly at the foot of the escalator.

'I'll try the Sanctuary first,' Aiden said, getting out his phone, 'and then the Trinovantum Council.'

As he made the call, something moved in the shadows and I saw we weren't alone. Three or four unshaven men and one woman were lying in sleeping bags on the floor.

'Artemis's Angels,' one of them said, striking a match so he could see us better. 'Come to give us an oracle.' He laughed softly. 'What shall we ask?'

'Do they serve beer in Hades?' suggested his friend, through a fit of coughing.

'This is it,' said the woman. Her voice was cultured, her face all bones and hollows. 'Welcome to the underworld.'

More people were squeezing their way through the entrance, seeking shelter. Even though there was plenty of space I felt crowded. The pressure in my head had intensified; my skin prickled and shivered.

'I don't . . . I don't feel very well,' I whispered.

'Maybe we should wait upstairs,' said Aiden, eyeing the new arrivals warily. He drew us back into the darker recesses of the foyer, then up the stairs to the first-floor gallery. I sank to the floor, my back against the door of a smashed-up accessories shop. *Orion's Belts.*

'Too highly strung, that's her problem,' Leto sniffed. 'All the girls are mollycoddled these days. It wasn't like that when I was a handmaiden.'

I tried to protest, and say that I was fine, really. But I couldn't. I couldn't even lift up my head. My body was crawling all over with dread.

Aura.

My head snapped upwards. 'Who was that?'

'Who was what?' Aiden asked.

'Who called my name?'

Aura.

Though the voice – and I thought it was a woman's – had spoken softly, its echo made the air shake. It was as if my skull was made of glass, and something had struck it to make it chime.

I squeezed my eyes shut, trying to calm the racing of my heart, to block out Aiden and Leto's confused faces, the restless sounds and movements in the darkness below.

But when I opened them again everything had changed.

*   *   *

I'd been here before. It seemed this was somewhere I'd known my whole life. A golden wood, a sky swollen with storm clouds. Someone or something was running ahead, flashing through the trees.

I could hear gasping, agonised breath. Not my own. A howl. Not my own either. Animal? Human –?

My body convulsed. I fell to my knees. The smell in my nostrils was of damp earth and rotting leaves. The trees' shadows lengthened and the moon rose.

Everything speeded up, sickeningly. The moon waxing and waning, clouds rushing across the sky, stars bursting to meet them. Dogs howling, my own breath sobbing, a high cold laughter. Hooves drummed through me. I was breaking into pieces, fragments of light and leaves.

Aura.

My name again. Said in a different voice.

The woods had gone. Aiden was holding me by the hands, saying my name, staring into my face. His own was frightened but his hands were firm and steady, and warm in mine.

'Do you see it?' I panted. 'Can you hear it?'

He began to speak but I shushed him. 'Listen,' I said. '*Listen.*'

More laughter, high and cold.

'The Green Knight,' I told him, though the voice wasn't my own. It was pure and ringing, and ancient as the night. 'The Green Knight will run red, for the march is stolen by the Iron Lord. He cries havoc, and the Python's Child shall preach with a double tongue –'

Darkness fell.

And then I was running, animal breath on my heels, the snap of their teeth on my skin. I was the hunter. I was the hunted. The moon spun in the sky. A man leaped before me, antlers bursting from his skull.

I felt the jaws of the hounds fasten on me. They dragged the voice out of my bone and flesh, the pit of my heart.

Forced out of my twisted, broken mouth –

A howl, like a beast's –

Like a man in agony, a woman in triumph.

I blacked out. When I came to, blinking and mumbling, the first thing I saw was Leto's wrinkled face staring into mine.

'Are you hurt?' she was asking.

I put my hand up to my mouth. There was blood on it. Otherwise I felt fine. I've never been drunk but I thought this might be what it was like. I was floppy and giddy, emptied out.

I looked for Aiden. He was hanging back in the shadows.

'What happened?'

'I don't . . . I don't know . . .' His face was strained and white. 'Those things you said . . . I don't understand . . .'

The old priestess got to her feet, her joints creaking, and pulled me up after her. 'The Trinovantum Council are sending a car to take us home. It'll be here any moment.'

'Leto . . . Tell me. Was I –? Did I –?'

'You got overexcited and had a funny turn. That's all.' She was busy tweaking my veil. Light flooded the foyer, followed by authoritative voices, the crackle of a radio.

Aiden stared at her. 'You don't believe that.'

Leto rounded on him with a savagery that made both of us start. 'Enough,' she hissed. 'Nothing happened. You heard nothing. There's nothing more to say.'

'But –'

'It's for your own good, but most of all hers. Aura –' She stopped, took a deep breath. 'Aura can't be seen running around the city with young men. Especially idiots like you. So stay back and keep your mouth shut. We're going home.'

Aiden tried to say something else, then stopped. Like me, he'd heard the note of fear in the old lady's voice, underneath the fierceness.

Shakily, Leto and I descended the stairs. There were two brawny policemen waiting to clear our way but people kept back of their own accord, murmuring uneasily. I wondered what they had heard and what, if anything, they would make of it.

'Leto,' I whispered, as we got into the car. 'The voice . . . whatever . . . whoever it was, it was . . . *real*.'

She shook her head. 'It doesn't matter. Trust me, it won't do you any good.'

CHAPTER 6

Back at the Sanctuary, there was nobody to tell even if I'd wanted to. Opis was attending a reception at the Royal Opera House, along with Cally and a couple of other priestesses.

'Go sleep it off,' Leto said as we parted. 'Don't cause trouble for yourself.' I was too on-edge and exhausted to argue.

As I lay in bed, my head still echoing and body humming, I touched my lips, remembering the taste of blood, and a tremor ran through my spine. *Green Knight* . . . *Python's Child* . . . *Iron Lord* . . . The words might as well have been in a foreign language. An alien tongue.

I was afraid to go to sleep. What if the hounds came for me again? I tossed and turned, imagining I could still hear the snap of their teeth, feel their hot animal breath on my skin. When Cally came in around midnight I closed my eyes and burrowed into the bedcovers so I wouldn't have to deal with her. The next thing I knew, it was morning.

I watched Cally move about, humming under her breath, her face lit up with that private glow again. It didn't trouble me. The tremors had gone; I felt calm, detached. There was no question of heeding Leto's muddled warnings – my destiny was in Artemis's hands. She'd given me an oracle and I was going to be High Priestess.

I wanted to see Opis before breakfast, but her PA told me she had already left for a meeting. I would have to wait until lunch.

In the meantime, I headed for the staff accommodation block. That's usually the best place to get news – either from newspapers and magazines left in the bins, or else from overheard conversations. I was in luck: two of the cooks were on a cigarette break. Cally and I discovered long ago that their smoking area was the best place for eavesdropping; it even has an ivy-shrouded wall to hide behind.

'. . . She fell down in a shopping centre,' the younger cook was saying, 'and started prophesying the End of Days.'

'Well, the Goddess Squad do like their shopping,' said her mate.

'No, I'm serious – it was on the radio this morning. A priestess, it was. There were witnesses and everything. One of 'em said she heard an animal howl and this really creepy laughter. I dunno about the prophecy, though . . . something about snakes and metal men.'

The other woman laughed. 'What, like *robots*?'

I would have liked to listen longer, but I was afraid of getting caught. As the morning wore on, my sense of calm deserted me. I wondered if the goddess would give me another oracle, and whether I wanted her to. I wondered if Opis could make sense of the words spoken through me.

On the way to see her, I passed Cynthia loitering on the lawn. She was the priestess who tried to run away. She used to be very pretty but there was something not quite right about her: she was too wispy and watery and, aged twenty-two, still sucked her thumb. 'Woo-hoo, Opis is after you!' she said in a babyish sing-song voice. I ignored her. Everyone does.

As I rang the bell on the Residence, I remembered my worries about the dinner party. They seemed so childish now. By the time I was shown into Opis's salon, my palms were sweaty and mouth was dry. She was sitting at her desk, in her most formal suit (Armani, navy) and most intimidating headdress (spiked, jet).

'I've already spoken to Leto and Aiden Carlyle this morning,' she said crisply, and without preamble. 'Now I'd like to hear your version of events.'

Haltingly, I tried to explain the impossible. 'Well, um . . . Artemis and I . . . the goddess, that is . . . the goddess spoke to me? And she gave me an oracle?'

I had no idea why everything I said sounded like a question. The sceptical expression on Opis's face just made everything worse. Every word I tried was clumsy and inadequate.

'Leto and Aiden think you were ill,' Opis said when I had finished. 'They believe it was some kind of panic attack. After all, you were in a highly stressful situation.'

I was prepared for Leto's treachery, even though I didn't understand it. But what was Aiden's game? I'd seen the shock and awe on his face; I'd heard it in his voice. I was sure he didn't believe I was hysterical – did he?

'Honoured Lady, I know it must have seemed strange – crazy even – to people on the outside. I can only say that what I felt, and saw, and heard wasn't like anything I've ever experienced. I don't understand it, but I *know* it was real. As real as me standing here and talking to you now.'

My voice trembled, but Opis didn't respond. Argos stirred in his corner by the window and let out a plaintive whine.

I waited some more. 'Don't you . . . don't you believe me?'

'Dear Aura,' Opis said at last, in the same cool tone as before, 'I've always thought your judgement sound. And I'm sure you're sincere. My main concern is the issue of information management. We don't want the rumours to run wild.'

'What do you think it meant? The Green Knight and the Iron Lord who cries –'

'Certainly, the matter requires careful consideration. That's why I must forbid you to speak to anyone about it. It will take time to form an appropriate response. There can be no room for error.'

Our High Priestess was right to be cautious. If I was going to be appointed her successor, she needed to make absolutely sure I was telling the truth.

I just wished that she could have acted a little more warmly, been a little less remote. It was almost as if she didn't *want* to believe me. Maybe she thought Cally would have been a more worthy recipient of Artemis's prophecy. Maybe Opis thought it should have come to her, as High Priestess, instead.

For the first time, I started to wonder how Opis might feel about giving up her powers. Unease prickled at my neck.

I went to the archive, but Leto refused to see me. Phoebe was there to give me the message that my services were no longer required. There was no sign of Aiden. I remembered the firm warmth of his hands, the shake in his voice when he said my name. He was denying his own experience as well as mine. He and Leto were as bad as each other, I fumed. Traitors and cowards.

Whatever 'information management' Opis was operating behind the scenes, it didn't seem to be entirely successful. Several hours before evening prayers, a boisterous crowd started to collect outside the temple. Many were clutching the little goddess dolls sold in the temple gift shop, and others had brought offerings – home-made cupcakes, cheap jewellery, bottles of wine. After a TV news crew arrived to report on the scene, the Trinovantum Council sent a squad of minders to escort us from the

74

Sanctuary as we made our way to the temple for weeknight prayers.

The priestesses kept trying to shush the hand-maidens' whispers and fidgets, even though they were as unsettled as everyone else. Rumours were flying, but nobody knew for sure what was involved. Or who. Most of the cult had been out and about yesterday; Leto and I weren't the only ones to have been caught up in the disturbances. Cally was in an extra-specially snappish mood.

Just you wait, I thought.

I watched the High Priestess make the libations of wine. Behind her, Artemis's statue rose up through a blue cloud of incense. To compare it or any other representation of the goddess to what I'd experienced was like holding up a child's drawing of the sea to an actual ocean. What if the goddess visited me here and now? I felt sick and shivery at the thought.

An oracle is supposed to take place in the temple, after the proper rites have been performed. A question is asked and an answer given. A direct revelation is much rarer. One of the most famous examples was in 1665, when a handmaiden of nine years of age foresaw the Great Plague and ensured the evacuation of the cult; she was made High Priestess at the age of ten and lived to the age of thirty, but never gave another oracle of value. I'd shown her prophecy to Aiden, I remembered, with a returning wrench of anger at how he'd betrayed mine.

There was generally a low turnout for weeknight prayers. It was a full house tonight. After the show ended and our visitors had reluctantly shuffled out, we waited, as usual, for our High Priestess's closing address. The silence throbbed with expectation.

'My dear friends,' she began, stepping up to the dais, 'I have always known my position in this cult is both a privilege and a duty. I am a servant of the goddess, just the same as you.

'The gift of prophecy is as mysterious as it is precious. Our mortal flesh is weak; our minds are clouded and easily confused. When I pray to Artemis to guide the words of my oracles, I tremble before her glory.

'Yet sometimes even divine inspiration is not enough to show us the way. In the midst of confusion and despair, we long for the miracle of revelation. I am here to tell you that such a revelation has occurred. One of our number has been called by the goddess herself.'

She paused to let her audience react. I was grateful that we were veiled. I sucked in my breath along with the rest of them.

'Her oracle will soon be shared with you all. For now, though, I wish to protect the identity of the prophetess. She needs to prepare herself to face the wider world and the demands it will make on her. And so I ask that you refrain from speculation and gossip. These are miraculous days and we must strive to be worthy of them. May Artemis Selene, Holy Lady of the Moon, inspire us all.'

We filed out of the temple in silence, the tension crackling between us like static. It wouldn't be long before the guessing games began, but nobody wanted to be the first to be caught speaking out of turn.

I should have been reassured by Opis's speech, yet there had been something in its tone that made me ill at ease, something slightly overblown. 'I tremble before her glory . . .' Is that how she spoke on important occasions, or had I only just started to notice it? I had no idea how I was supposed to prepare to 'face the wider world' either. Opis had her own PR rep and press officer. Why weren't they, or anyone else, coming to talk to me?

At least I wouldn't have to face Cally. Tomorrow was her sixteenth birthday, the day she would be initiated as a priestess, and she was spending the time before the ceremony in isolation, fasting and prayer. Afterwards, she'd move into her own room. Just a few weeks ago, the two of us had enjoyed a rare moment of harmony when we'd picked out the wallpaper and bed linen for our new priestess rooms. I'd been so excited by the prospect of an en-suite bathroom . . . It seemed like another life.

The following day the Sanctuary was besieged by journalists and miracle-seekers. Nobody was allowed in or out. The newspapers weren't delivered to the handmaidens' sitting room until twelve, when I pushed ahead of the younger girls to get first look. As usual, some articles had been cut out, but on this occasion we were only interested in one news item. AN ORACLE AWAKENS? was *The Times*'s headline. The cult's press release was pretty much a summary of what Opis had said in the temple last night and was followed by a statement of support from the Trinovantum Council. Then came the oracle itself.

My oracle.

Except it wasn't, quite.

The Green Knight will run red, but the match will
be saved by the Iron Lord. He arises from havoc, and
the Python's Child shall preach until the troubles
are done.

The next moment the newspaper was snatched from me and passed around, the other girls exclaiming and gasping, debating who the lucky handmaiden or priestess might be. The favourites were Cynthia, because she was odd, and Cally, because she looked the part. I barely heard any of it. There was a rushing and whirring in my head.

'Honoured Lady, I don't understand. These aren't the words of my prophecy –'

I'd rushed over to the Residence and into the Gold Room without even waiting for the maid to announce me. Opis and Lionel Winter were going over the accounts, sitting close together and laughing about something. When they saw me standing before them, they abruptly straightened up. Lionel Winter gave me his flintiest stare.

Opis, however, didn't look angry. She spoke slowly and calmly, as if to a wayward child.

'There were witnesses to your oracle, Aura. Reliable ones.'

'Witnesses? Do you mean Aiden and Leto?'

'Yes. They've made an official statement.'

'But – but you said they didn't believe me – they thought I was having a panic attack –'

'Whatever they thought of your state of mind, they were quite clear as to what they heard you say.'

I tried to speak again, but Lionel Winter talked over me.

'You were possessed by a god,' he said. 'Your mind was assaulted, your senses scattered. It's not surprising your memories of the event are confused.'

'Exactly.' Opis leaned forward, took on a confiding tone. 'When I give the oracle, I hardly know day from night, up from down. That's why the Lord Herne is by my side when I receive the goddess. I need someone to bear witness, as well as help interpret the prophecy.'

I bit my lip. It felt as if the words I'd spoken had been seared into my brain:

The Green Knight will run red, for the march is stolen by the Iron Lord. He cries havoc, and the Python's Child shall preach with a double tongue.

'March is stolen' was very different to 'match will be saved'. And the phrase 'until the troubles are done' was more clunky, if less mysterious, than 'double tongue' . . . I pressed my hands to my eyes, trying to recall every last detail of my vision.

'I can't forget what I heard. I'm certain I got the words right.'

'Events will decide,' Lionel replied. 'After all, your prediction has yet to be fulfilled.'

'If and when it's been proven,' said Opis sweetly, 'we'll talk again. That's when we will present you to the world, and you can tell your story however you wish.'

I shook my head in frustration. 'By then it will be too late. The prophecy's a warning – I'm sure of it. If we can just work out –'

Lionel held up his hand to silence me. 'The High Priestess and I have extensive experience of interpreting the words of the goddess. It would be presumptuous of you to even attempt the task.'

'Besides,' said Opis, 'you have other responsibilities to attend to. Callisto is dedicating herself to the cult today, and your own initiation is the day after tomorrow.' She smiled, though her eyes were flat and cold. 'Whatever the future holds, dear Aura, it's the present you should be concerned with.'

CHAPTER 7

The first part of my oracle came true the next evening. It was announced by a shrieking storm of police and ambulance sirens, but they were so common these days we barely noticed. And all the handmaidens were preoccupied anyway, with preparing Cally for her initiation.

It began with a bath. There was a room in the depths of Artemisia House that had been specially built for this purpose. It was meant to evoke the mystic grotto where the goddess bathed with her nymphs, and has a kind of marble paddling pool in the centre, surrounded by potted ferns. The walls were painted with scenes of ancient Greek nymphs as imagined by the late Victorians, all plump pink flesh and rosebud mouths.

We rigged up curtains round the pool to give Cally some privacy, and put tea lights among the greenery.

Although the water came from a London tap, we added a few drops that were bottled at the sacred spring in Delphi in Greece. We were supposed to sing choral odes as the initiate splashes about, though without Cally to keep us in tune it was all bit creaky.

When she emerged, bathed and dressed, it was to a chorus of admiring coos. She was wearing a white silk tunic, fastened with gold pins at the shoulder, and a gold girdle round her waist. Her veil was crowned by a wreath of white asphodel and dark purple amaranths. After the ceremony, she would be presented with a priestess's mantle of violet wool with a silver trim.

I scanned Cally's face for signs of anxiety. She must be worrying about the oracle, and people's reaction once they found out it wasn't her. She was upright and stiff, with two spots of colour high on her cheeks. But that just showed she was taking her initiation with the proper seriousness.

Although the service wasn't open to the general public, the Sacred Hall was full to bursting. Cally's mother was in the front row, wearing a dangerously low-cut top. She kept dabbing at her eyes throughout the ceremony, collagen-swollen lips quivering with emotion. Most of the Trinovantum Council had turned up. Seb was there, and Aiden too.

This really surprised me. What was in it for him? It occurred to me that he'd made some deal with Opis and the council, in return for reducing his community service. That would explain his behaviour over my oracle. Bitterness flooded me – so much for his high-minded, man-of-the-people act. I wanted to catch his eye to glare at him but he spent the whole time staring stiffly at the floor.

Health and safety regulations, not to mention animal rights, had put a stop to the traditional sacrifice of a white hart, so we handmaidens had baked a honey-cake in the shape of a deer to place on the altar as an offering. It was the priestesses who would lead Callisto down to the crypt and deliver her to the Seat of the Oracle.

I tried to imagine the same thing happening to me on my own birthday, the day after tomorrow. It didn't feel real. I couldn't concentrate on anything but the words of the prophecy, and how far I could trust my own mind. Or how far I could trust Opis . . . Perhaps I should have paid more attention when Aiden had made references to her ruthlessness. But he was a liar, I told myself. I should forget all about him.

After the ceremony was finished, we returned to the Sanctuary, and discovered the reason for all those emergency service sirens.

'Sir Alan Greendale's been assassinated,' one of the

cleaners told us breathlessly. 'Gunned down, right outside the Royal Courts of Justice!'

'The Green Knight!' somebody cried out, amid exclamations and gasps.

Sir Alan Greendale was the chair of the Electoral Commission, which had condemned the recent election as being 'riddled with abuses'.

The Green Knight will run red.

I closed my eyes, visualised blood pouring from gunshot wounds. I knew at that moment I should never have doubted my vision, or my memory of it. My first reaction was guilt. Something that had been predicted should have been prevented. My second reaction was anger – at Opis and Lionel. Why hadn't they listened to me? Why hadn't they *done* something?

Meanwhile, the cult crowded around the TV in the priestesses' sitting room. Although we aren't given internet access, we are permitted to watch a select number of TV channels, and BBC News is one of them. They reported that the assassin was a lone gunman who had escaped on motorcycle. Nobody was pointing the finger . . . yet. But it seemed clear the prime minister couldn't survive this latest crisis, even though the main opposition party was split by infighting of its own.

The newsreaders adopted a slightly uncomfortable, jocular tone when they referenced the oracle. The religious correspondent said that a representative from the cult was expected to make a statement this evening. In the meantime, he observed that 'many people will now be scouring the prophecy for clues as to Sir Alan's killer, and the identity of the Iron Lord – the one who would save the match'.

My guilt increased. Only I knew that the prophecy was untrue, or rather mistaken.

The fate of the Green Knight had already revealed itself. The only other part I felt sure of was the Python's Child. Python must be a reference to the Pythia, the ancient Oracle of Delphi, who was named after the snake that was killed by the god Apollo. Our own oracle was therefore her 'child' and heir. *The Python's Child shall preach* . . . That seemed to suggest there would be more prophecies to come. But would they be given to Opis or me or someone else entirely? Could the man who threw snakes at the festival be somehow involved? The 'double tongue' was most likely a warning – the oracles of legend were full of double meanings.

Opis must still be occupied with Cally and might not even have heard the news. Even so, I felt increasingly unsettled as time went on and no message came to me from the Residence.

The priestess on night duty checked I was in my room at ten, but didn't say anything except to wish me good-night. I lay alone in the darkness, missing the quiet breathing and murmurings of the other girls, wondering when the call would come . . . and what Opis had planned for me. I couldn't escape the feeling that something was very wrong.

Still sleepless at midnight, I got up and sat by the window. I thought of all the other people dreaming in this house, all the other people lying wakeful and restless in this city. I wondered if the goddess watched over them too.

Then I saw Opis outside the Sanctuary gates. She was hooded, but her figure was unmistakable in the glow of the street lamp. I couldn't see the face of the man she was with, but from his height and pale hair guessed it must be the Lord Herne. Before I could think better of it, I grabbed a coat and hurried downstairs. I knew where the key to the side door was hidden. I was quick: by the time I got outside, Opis and the Lord Herne were just saying their goodbyes. I waited for her in the covered passageway that led through Artemisia House to the garden beyond.

She was on her phone. 'Yes, I've just spoken to him,' she said crisply. 'We're confident we can contain the situation. In fact, it may well work to our advantage. The girl won't cause any trouble, I assure you.'

She put the phone back in her pocket just as I stepped out of the shadows. 'Honoured Lady.' I touched my hand to my brow, a little breathless at my own daring. 'I need to speak with you.'

I didn't mean to startle her, but she drew back with a hiss. Her slanting eyes glittered under the hood.

'What? What is it you want, Aura? What do you think you know?'

'I know the oracle everyone's talking about is the wrong –'

She put a hand on my arm. The gesture looked gentle, but her grip was iron as she pulled me into the darkness of the passageway.

'Be very careful, Aura. Choose your words wisely.'

'It's just – the news – the Green Knight, the assassination – it proves my prophecy was real, *true*, but it's the wrong version out there. I'm sure of it. We have to put it right, so people *know*.'

She laughed. It wasn't a laugh I'd heard before. It was sharp, sour.

'Oh, Aura. You've been listening behind closed doors, haven't you? Sneaking and spying, spinning your little webs. And now lurking in the dark to ambush me . . . Do you take me for a fool?'

'N-never, Honoured Lady!' I stammered. 'I only want people to know what the goddess said to me. The goddess –'

She gave another low hiss. 'Don't presume to lecture me about the goddess.' Her nails dug deep into the flesh of my arm. 'I am her oracle and High Priestess. You're nothing, a nobody, and it will be far better for you if you stay that way. Because I'm warning you, Aura, the kind of attention you're after can be very dangerous. Understand?'

I nodded. I was too shocked to do anything else.

Opis took a step back. This time, her smile was almost friendly. 'I'm sorry to see this change in you. You used to be such a good girl – so quiet and dutiful. That's the girl I want to see at your initiation. Perhaps a period of silence and reflection will help you find her again.'

She summoned over the night porter. All Sanctuary staff are female; those on security are ex-military or -police.

'Aura is going to prepare herself for her initiation a little ahead of time,' she told the woman. 'I'd like you to make sure she settles in.'

CHAPTER 8

The Quiet Room, set up as a retreat for stressed-out cult members and those preparing for important rituals, wouldn't be out of place in an upmarket spa. There were scented candles and white linen, and exotic fruit juices for those on a fast. I wasn't taken there.

Instead, I was marched into one of the attic bedrooms that used to be for the maids, before the staff block was built. It was stuffy and cramped, with a painted-in window; the only furnishings were a lumpy single bed and a bare light bulb. There was a toilet in the adjoining room, but no washbasin. I was locked in.

What was swelling in me frightened me – something black and boiling, utterly foreign. As I paced back and forth, fists clenched, I hardly recognised myself. Mousy little Aura. Shadowy little Aura. So meticulous in the archives, so dutiful in Greek class . . . And now, according to Opis, a rebel and spy. For one thing was clear: Opis didn't believe in my prophecy. She thought I'd overheard something I shouldn't have and she'd exploited it to cause trouble.

All my life, I'd put my faith in the comfort given by our oracles, the beauty of our rituals. Now I realised this wasn't enough. Our ceremonies had become too pretty, with their scented candles and choral songs, the purple prose. There was none of the stench and smoke of real sacrifice.

And maybe, I realised, there's no real prophecy either. Opis has no oracles and no faith, and she doesn't even care.

When morning light showed at the window, I tried to pray. I didn't know where to start. I had always wanted to be sure that I was doing the right thing. I had wanted to feel Chosen. Now I'd been chosen as the oracle, and it terrified me. There was no doubt that if I failed my duty to Artemis I was marked out for a far worse punishment than anything Opis could devise.

That didn't mean I wasn't worried about Opis's plans. *We're confident we can contain the situation*, she'd said on the phone. *The girl won't cause any trouble.* Was she talking about me? All I'd done was speak the truth. But somehow the truth was getting in Opis's way. Not just hers either. I sensed 'the situation' was bigger than both of us.

I kept replaying the accusations of the man who'd interrupted the festival speeches, the one who knew Opis's Christian name. I wondered what had happened to him after he was dragged away.

The day wore on. I grew hungrier, thirstier, sweatier. The heat in the room had become stifling. I couldn't turn off the radiator, which had been set to high.

At half past six in the evening, the key turned in the lock. I stiffened all over. Opis, come to see the effects of her punishment.

But it was Cally. She had a bottle of water for me.

I was so surprised I didn't say anything. Neither did she, at first. Her face was very pale. She was holding the floral garland from her initiation ceremony and plucked at it nervously.

'How are you?' she asked at last.

'I'm . . . OK. Opis is angry with me.'

'She says you've been pretending to be the one who had the oracle.' Cally sounded almost offhand about it.

'That's not true.'

'Of course it can't be you,' she said calmly. 'That would be ridiculous. You are unworthy.'

'Did Opis send you to talk to me?'

'No. I shouldn't be here. So now that I am I don't want to hear any more of your blasphemy.'

'It *was* me who had the oracle, Cally. I swear it. I saw –'

She put her hands over her ears. 'Stop it. You're delusional. Anyway, that's not what I came to talk about. I –' She gave a pinched sort of smile. 'Are you looking forward to your initiation?'

'I suppose so.' I waited, but she didn't respond. 'Did you, er, enjoy yours? Was it what you expected?'

'Yes. I don't know. I think . . .' Cally sat down on the bed, wilted garland in her lap. Dead purple petals fell on to the floor. Amaranths – or love-lies-bleeding, as it's more commonly known. She bit her lip. 'I think the goddess might be angry with me.'

'The goddess? Why?'

She spoke in a rush that became a gabble, so that I strained to hear the words. 'It was my choice. I told myself it was what they all wanted. Opis, the Lord Herne, the council . . . and therefore the goddess must want it too. But now I think I was fooling myself. Because it was me who wanted it, really, deep down, and I let the others persuade me to make myself feel better.

And now I think that it was wrong, after all, and the goddess will punish me.'

'Why? What have you done?'

And why was she confessing to me, of all people? But, though she coloured all over, she didn't answer.

I tried again. 'What are you worried about? Arrows and thunderbolts and transformations? That doesn't happen any more. It's like most religious stories. They're . . . metaphors.'

I knew how hypocritical I was being. The woman in my vision was capable of thunderbolts, all right. But Cally was frightened, and I'd never seen that before.

During the sacred rituals, she was always aquiver with attentiveness. She'd give an occasional nod, as if to reassure the goddess that her instructions were coming through loud and clear. When she stood before the altar, you could practically smell the holiness rolling off her in incense-scented waves. I'd always thought it was for show. Was it possible, in spite of all her theatrics and posturing, that Cally really did believe?

'The gods are vengeful,' she whispered. 'People are vengeful. Do you remember that trip we had, when we were eleven, to the old punishment place?'

I nodded. We'd been taken to see the underground

chamber where priestesses who broke their vows or betrayed the cult used to be buried alive. It's a small stone room, sunk deep into the ground of the cult cemetery in Southwark.

'It was so dark in there. It felt like even the air above it was stained.' Cally shivered and rubbed her arms. 'I used to have nightmares of being left there as they shovelled the earth in.'

'It scared me too. But that place hasn't been used for over a hundred years. We live in more civilised times. People don't get tortured or executed any more.'

'Yes, and look what a mess the country's in.' Her face hardened; suddenly, she was back to her righteously superior self. 'Maybe people *need* to be frightened. Maybe you can't have true faith without fear.' She grasped my hand with chilly fingers. 'And there are still all sorts of punishments, even now.'

Was she threatening me or warning me? I couldn't tell.

'Cally – Callisto, I mean – what's all this about?'

'Nothing. It doesn't matter. I'm just saying it would be better for you if you did as you were told.' She got up from the bed. 'It's for your own good, I promise.'

She reached into her pockets and brought out a

handful of biscuits. 'Don't let anyone know I gave these to you.'

Then she was gone.

More hours passed. I fell into a fitful doze for some of them. At six o'clock in the morning, a terrible banging and crashing commenced on the other side of the wall. Workmen were starting some kind of renovation. The noise carried on, with little respite, for the rest of the day. Happy birthday to me.

I had tried to eke out the biscuits and the water but they didn't last long. My stomach was hollow with hunger, my mouth dry with thirst. My head ached. I was sure the noise next door was part of the punishment. As the shadows lengthened, I began to wonder how long I would be left here. Days? Weeks? Months? Until I agreed to say and do whatever I was told?

But at half past seven the door opened again. Fat Atalanta was there, pink and breathless, and holding a clean tunic and a Thermos of soup. So I'd been forgiven, or at least reprieved. They were still going to let me become a priestess.

I lay, lapped by water, in the marble basin. Through a gap in the curtains, I saw one of the nymphs on the wall, peeping coyly from behind a cypress tree. There were only five handmaidens, now, to sing the choral odes, and after a half-hearted verse or two they'd given up and were whispering and giggling among themselves.

Once I was dressed, the girls clustered around, trying to *ooh* and *ahh* with appropriate enthusiasm. I could tell they were struggling. In the mirror they gave me, I saw new hollows in my cheeks, and dark rings round my eyes.

The temple was half empty for the ceremony. People had come for Callisto because of the rumours that she was the girl who'd had the oracle. I was a nobody, as Opis said. Once, this wouldn't have particularly mattered. This place was the only home, and family, I'd ever known or needed. But as I walked into the smoky glitter of the Sacred Hall I felt a stranger in a strange land.

As I finished the purification rituals – sprinkling the altar with holy water, brushing dust from the dais with a broom of cypress boughs – I glanced up and saw Aiden in the front row. It was enough to temporarily jolt me out of my daze. He stared back, expressionless. He wasn't in his usual ill-fitting, grungy clothes. His suit was as sharp as his cheekbones. His shaggy hair was sleeked back. Every inch the Trinovantum Councillor.

It was a relief to turn away from him and take my place in front of the statue of Artemis. The High Priestess picked up her ceremonial silver arrow and held its point to my heart.

'Do you vow to honour the laws of the temple and this land?'

Opis's gaze was as serene as the marble woman who loomed behind us. For a moment, I wondered if I'd imagined our midnight meeting in the passageway. Then I felt the metal point of the arrow press through the thin silk, right against my skin.

'I do, lest I suffer the arrows of Artemis and the waters of the Styx.'

The Lord Herne stepped forward with an impatient swish of his green velvet cloak.

'Do you vow to serve the goddess in all her rites and works?'

Lionel Winter passed me a shard of rock, a symbol of Troy's fallen walls, and folded my hand tightly round its jagged edge. His eyes burned into me from under the antler headdress.

'I do, for I am bound by the blood of King Brutus and the stones of Troy.'

On it went. Question and answer, promise and threat.

I hardly knew what I was saying but I must have made the right responses, for at the end the Lord Herne led me to where the sacred fire flickered in its brazier, and guided my hand as I put a taper to the flame. The other priestesses gathered to form an escort as I carried the taper through the door behind the altar, down the dark stairs to the crypt below. I was bringing the light of the goddess into the underworld. As the door closed behind us, I heard the handmaidens raise their voices in the final song.

In the crypt, I stood in front of the rough slab of stone that was King Brutus's altar. The narrow opening to the Chamber of the Oracle was in the wall opposite, concealed by a curtain. What was waiting for me there? Above ground was a sprawling modern city of concrete and neon and exhaust fumes. Below, I could be standing in the temple at Troy. The shrine at Delphi. The gateway to Hades.

I carried the only source of light; the darkness around me was filled with the rustlings of robed women: Opis, Leto, Aphaea, Cynthia, Amarysia, Atalanta, Aeginaea, Aetole, Agrotera, Callisto . . . Familiar faces made strange by the shadows.

Leto, as the oldest priestess, fastened my new mantle to my shoulders, with her usual scowl. It *won't do you any good*, she'd told me. She'd been right, and I still didn't understand why. One by one, the others stepped forward to kiss me on the cheek. When it was Cally's turn, I felt her fingers close briefly and tightly round my wrist. I couldn't tell if this was a blessing or warning. Cynthia was blinking and shivering. I felt a shudder of my own run down my back.

Finally the others withdrew. I was alone with the High Priestess and the Lord Herne. In spite of myself, the hand holding the taper shook.

One of the priestesses had brought down a gold chalice and set it on the altar. Opis lifted its lid and steam rose into the air. There was a smell of wine and honey. With the point of the gold arrow, she made a cut in her wrist, and let a couple of drops of blood fall into the cup.

'The gods' veins run with ichor,' she intoned. 'And mortal veins run with blood. They drink nectar, and we drink wine. Blood to ichor, wine to nectar, human to divine. Tonight, you will face the miracle of metamorphosis.'

'What . . . what is my task?'

'To guard the goddess's light and tend her flame. The rest is for Artemis to reveal.'

Then she reached out and stroked my cheek. 'Dear Aura,' she said, 'you are so nearly one of us. I hope you have been thinking about what we discussed. I am sure you have prayed for guidance.'

'I have, Honoured Lady.'

'So do you renounce your false prophecy?'

She spoke so tenderly that in spite of myself, tears sprang to my eyes.

'I – I can't, Honoured Lady.' I licked my cracked lips. 'I don't want to make you angry. But I have to speak the truth. My prophecy was real.'

The High Priestess sighed, soft and low.

'It is your choice,' she murmured. 'Remember that.'

The Lord Herne lifted the cup to my lips. I saw his cufflinks glint from under the green cloak. The reflected flame danced in his eyes. I hesitated, just for a moment, and then I drank.

CHAPTER 9

I'd gone more than forty-eight hours with hardly anything to eat and very little sleep. I'd been feeling faint all day. But this weakness was different. My limbs had suddenly become slow. The taper I was holding had become almost unbearably heavy. Everything seemed very small and far away.

I don't even remember going through the curtain and into a second stone room. The Chamber of the Oracle. Through bleary eyes I saw an alcove that had been carved out of a wall of sheer rock. The alcove contained a small statue. It was Artemis Selene, Lady of the Moon, veiled, with a crescent moon as her crown. But it was nothing like the elaborately carved sculpture in the temple. It was worn and crude, smoke-blackened. This was the goddess that had been carried out of the ruins of Troy.

I walked unsteadily towards the statue. There was a bronze tripod seat in front of it next to an unlit brazier on a stand. A dish was set above the coals, containing dried leaves or herbs of some kind. In the wall on my right was a small door, also of polished bronze. It was locked.

I must light the fire, I told myself. I must tend the sacred flame. I must think good thoughts about the goddess and her cult, and then Opis and Artemis wouldn't be angry with me any more. When the kindling caught light and the coals began to glow, tears of relief filled my eyes. Maybe everything was going to be all right.

I climbed on to the tripod. It felt precariously high. The heat from the brazier soon caused the dish of leaves to smoke, releasing a heavy herbal scent into the room. I don't know how long I sat there, gazing at the goddess, woozily soaking up the warmth. It could have been ten minutes or two hours. I closed my eyes.

I awoke from my sleep or trance or whatever it was with a start. Panic seized me. For a moment I didn't know where I was.

Even when I remembered, it made no sense. There was a draught blowing through the room and the fire had gone out. Yet the darkness was filled with smoke; I could smell it on me, and the air had a strange thickness to it. I thought of Troy again, of burning houses, charred flesh. I thought of the dank black hole that was the place of punishment.

I'd failed my initiation. I'd failed the goddess. I was going to Hades –

But there, after all, was a small spark in the blackness. A fleck of light. Something was moving in the smoke.

I clambered down from my seat. I thought I heard footsteps and staggered after them, tripping up on my mantle, my garland slipping crookedly down over my eyes. I must catch the light, save the fire... Shape-shifting wraiths loomed out of the darkness, before falling back and dissolving into smoke. My ears rang and my breath rasped.

I found a gap in the wall. I groped for the curtain, and touched cool metal instead. The little bronze door was now open. There was a curved passage beyond. Was this another part of the initiation? How far did the crypt go?

I stumbled forward, following the light. No longer was it a small guttering flame, but a steady glow. It was coming from another door along the passageway, which had been left ajar.

The ringing in my ears was deafening. The smoke swirled in my head. I didn't want to go on. But the door was already opening.

A green man, with the head of a stag, stood on the threshold of a forest.

I shrank back. I remembered my vision of the golden wood. The leaping, twisting body . . . the antlers springing from the skull . . . Metamorphosis, as Opis had promised. Or was it? My mouth tasted sour. Chemical.

I needed to run, like a hunted animal. I was sweating and panting, yet frozen to where I stood. Trapped prey.

The stag-man advanced upon me. The trees behind him flickered. It was a room covered in leaves. Painted leaves. Through the flickering and the fog, I saw an oil lamp and frescoed walls, a carved wooden bed. As the man drew me into the room, I tried to push him off and grabbed a fistful of velvet cloak. My hands were too weak to hold on to it. A new terror rose in my throat. I knew the goddess wasn't here. I wasn't possessed. I'd been poisoned.

The man had me by the wrist, was leading me towards the bed as I struggled limply in his grasp. My screams were trapped in my lungs; I was choking on them.

'It's OK, it's OK. Hush. Aura, please . . .'

I recognised the antler headdress and the cloak. They belonged to the Lord Herne. This wasn't Lionel Winter, though. It was a boy with green eyes and tangled hair. The poison was everywhere. Everything was infected.

'Get – *away* – *from* – *me* –'

He let go. I lurched into a corner of the room, where I crouched on the floor, arms wrapped round my knees, stiff and shuddering.

'Aura, it's me. Aiden. I'm not going to hurt you, I promise. I'm here to help.'

He removed the headdress and knelt down beside me. I flinched away.

'Listen to me, Aura. You've been drugged. You're ill. I can make you better, but you have to trust me. Here.' There was a little pink pill in his hand. 'Take it. It's medicine – an anti-hallucinogenic. It will help.'

I shook my head, so the room dipped and swayed, and the leaves on the wall seemed to rustle. His voice became more urgent.

'I'm going to get you out of here, Aura, and take you somewhere safe. But we have to make you better first. You have to trust me.'

'Why . . . why . . . should I?'

He took a deep breath. 'Because I believe in you. I believe in your oracle.'

We stared at each other.

'Please, Aura. Take the pill.'

In the end, I was too exhausted to go on resisting.

Afterwards, I lay curled on the stone floor, eyes closed, for what felt like a lifetime. Time slowed; so did the racing of my heart. My mouth still tasted of chemicals. But when I opened my eyes again, the painted forest was flat and motionless, and the smoke had cleared. Aiden was sitting at the end of the bed, chewing his nails and staring at me anxiously.

'How did you get here?' I said at last. I couldn't raise my voice above a whisper.

'I volunteered. They – Opis and Lionel and the rest – think I'm one of them now. They think I'm part of it. But I came to help you escape. I've got a key – I can take you out the way I came in.'

'I can't leave the cult,' I said numbly.

'You have to.' Aiden sounded exasperated. Despite myself, tears rose in my eyes. I knew he was right.

'It's not safe for you here. They'll find a way of shutting you up, driving you crazy. Aura . . . they want to break you.'

'Why?' I whispered, though I already knew.

'Your prophecy is getting in their way. Look, I'll explain more later. But, if you're feeling strong enough, we need to get out of here. It's half past three now. Leto will be waiting.'

'Leto?'

'Yeah.' Aiden rumpled up his hair distractedly. 'She's the one who told me you were in trouble, and that I had to get in with the Council.'

He helped me to my feet and picked up the lamp. I wondered if that was the moving light I'd seen earlier. We walked out into the passageway, which curved away from the Chamber of the Oracle and went on for some distance underground. The stairs at its end took us out to a dark cul-de-sac just a couple of buildings down from the Trinovantum Council's clubhouse.

A hunched figure emerged from behind a skip. It was Leto. 'About time,' she harrumphed.

'Wait here,' Aiden told me, 'while I go get the car.'

Leto had brought me a small overnight bag, as well as an oversized hooded sweatshirt and tracksuit bottoms. In silence, I pulled them over my ridiculous costume, while she stuffed my mantle and garland into the skip. I knew the old priestess had taken a huge risk. I had so much I wanted to say to her, so many questions to ask. Yet I was so dazed I hardly knew how to start.

'Leto . . . if Aiden hadn't been there to help . . . what would have happened to me?'

'A wedding night,' she said brusquely. 'Of sorts. Between the council and the cult. Isn't it the usual remedy for troublesome girls? Find a man to put 'em in their place.'

I felt a wave of nausea. 'How – how –?'

'*Obviously* there's nothing like it in the true ritual. That would be an abomination.' She screwed up her face. 'Mind you, I doubt Opis was the first to think of it – the Trinovantum Council has a history of getting a bit too close to pretty priestesses.'

I thought of pretty Cynthia – how she tried to run away after becoming a priestess and hadn't been the same since. I thought of Cally's strange attempt at confession.

'Cally –'

'Callisto's deluded enough to fancy she's in love. She and Seb Winter will make a fine power-couple, just like Opis and Lionel before them. The girl's been groomed for stardom and she knows it. Don't you worry about her.'

I kept silent.

'Where's that boy got to?' Leto muttered. 'Flighty. That's his problem. *Both* of your problems. I told you not to cause trouble, didn't I?' she said, suddenly angry again. 'I warned you. And you never listened.'

'I had to speak the truth. I – I had no choice.'

'Hah. Such a meek little thing, you were. Nothing but milk and water in your veins. But you've a stubborn streak after all. A rebel spark. Just like your m–'

Her mouth abruptly clamped shut.

'What do you mean? Do you – did you – know my mother?'

She didn't answer. She didn't look at me either.

All the breath seemed to leave my body. 'Leto . . . was my mother . . . a priestess too?'

'It doesn't matter,' she mumbled. 'She's dead and gone, poor girl. Leave the dead alone.'

'Then . . . who was my father?'

She looked up, eyes glinting. 'Trouble, that's who. And see,' she said with evident relief, 'here's your knight in shining armour. It's time to go.'

'Leto –'

'Go. Before her Honoured Ladyship and Lionel come looking.'

She practically bundled me into the back seat of Aiden's beaten-up car. I tried to ask more questions but she was suddenly deaf. The car's engine was running and Aiden was tapping his hands impatiently on the wheel. 'What about you?' I managed to get out.

'What if Opis discovers you helped me?'

'Hmph. I know how to look after myself – which is more than can be said for you.'

With that, the old priestess slammed the door shut and shuffled away into the night. Aiden wasted no time in driving off.

'Where are we going?'

'Somewhere you'll be safe. Somewhere people will listen to you.'

He attempted a reassuring smile but his face was tense.

My shock was ebbing way, to be replaced by a hot and bloody rage. And, in spite of myself, the ache of bereavement. I had been betrayed by the only family I'd ever had, in the heart of the only home I'd ever known.

It wasn't just the horrors of the crypt. Leto's revelation was a different kind of betrayal: it exposed the fact that most of the people I'd grown up with had lied about who I was. I wasn't an anonymous orphan; I was the daughter of a priestess. In which case . . . could my father be one of those fat old Trinovantum Councillors I'd made chit-chat with over canapés? My skin crawled.

I had one comfort, however: nobody would be able to lie to me ever again. I had the power and authority of the oracle. I would broadcast the truth to the world. I would take revenge on the cult for myself and the goddess, and all the other people it had exploited and deceived. I would –

The car screeched to a halt. Aiden swore. I jolted upright, heart jumping. Had we been caught already?

But no – Aiden had braked because an animal was standing in front of us in the otherwise deserted road. In the glow of the headlights, it looked huge. A silver wolf with burning black eyes, staring right at us.

I screwed up my eyes, and when I looked again gave a hiccupy laugh of relief.

'Argos! He must have snuck out from the Sanctuary. Perhaps Leto left the gate open.'

Aiden stuck his head out of the window. 'Shoo! Go home! Bad dog!'

Argos didn't move. He raised his head, gave a low howl. The back of my neck tingled.

'He's coming with us,' I said.

'What? No, wait –'

Before Aiden could stop me or I could think better of it, I scrambled out of the car. Argos immediately trotted over. I opened the door to the back seat and he jumped in, with a little grunt of contentment. I squeezed in next to him.

Muttering, Aiden drove on. I leaned against the dog's warm furry bulk and closed my eyes. He nudged my cheek with his nose, huffing gently. I remembered the hunt in the golden wood. I remembered the hounds snapping at my heels. I knew why Argos had been sent to me. It was a sign of favour, but also a warning.

Maybe I could outrun Opis. I couldn't outrun the goddess.

CHAPTER 10

As he drove, Aiden filled me in on how he'd come to rescue me, talking quickly and nervously to fill the silence. I didn't take much in. Later, I got the story in full.

The morning after I'd given the oracle, Leto had telephoned Aiden to say that I was in serious trouble and needed somebody on the inside of the Trinovantum Council who would be able to look out for me. Almost immediately afterwards, he was summoned to a meeting with both Opis and Lionel, where they offered to make his community service and police record 'go away' if he'd cooperate with the cult.

'I've always been curious about what the cult and council get up to behind the scenes. So I also asked to be elected to the Trinovantum. Dear old Dad was so pleased his prodigal son had seen the light that he sealed the deal with a hefty donation.'

Though Aiden didn't make it explicit, it seemed the cash had also helped secure his place at my initiation. Leto had told him what might happen there too.

Aiden then explained how the smoke I'd inhaled had probably come from the same mix of laurel leaves and other opiates that Opis used to 'get in the mood' for the oracle, and it was the drugged wine that had had the most toxic effect. He'd got the anti-hallucinogenic pill off a friend of his who did some dealing on the side.

Aiden kept glancing at me in the mirror. I avoided his eye. I felt an overpowering mix of gratitude for his rescue of me and humiliation that he'd seen me in such a state, out of control of my own body and mind.

'I'm really sorry you had to go through that,' he said abruptly and, I thought, uncomfortably. 'It was . . . horrible.'

I realised he was embarrassed too.

'Thank you.' I had no other words. I was trying not to wonder what his instructions had been. I didn't want to think of that room – the high wooden bed, the painted forest – ever again.

Instead, I stared mindlessly out of the window. It was a damp night and the roads were oily with rain. There was hardly any traffic about and just a few lost souls huddled in doorways or weaved unsteadily through the puddles.

'I'm taking you to a safe house,' Aiden said. 'It's a retreat for people who aren't happy with the system, or need to keep their heads down for a while.'

'How do you know them?'

'I got into activism at school. Mostly to piss off my dad, if I'm honest. I'd wind him up over dinner with grand socialist theories. But the more I learned about what was going on in the world, the more I realised I had to do more than just whinge about stuff. So I joined some groups, went on demos. One thing led to another, I guess.'

'Your friends will let me join them?'

'They're expecting you. Leto and I weren't the only witnesses to your oracle. There were other people in the shopping centre, remember. Most couldn't see or hear you properly, and didn't know what was going on. But enough people were there for word to get out – word that contradicted the official oracle, that is. I think the Trinovantum Council bought off or intimidated the other witnesses. But one woman refused. She's in hiding too.'

Aiden turned the car into a wide residential street and swore. 'Crap. There's a checkpoint.'

'Is it . . . is it the cult?'

'Unlikely. I was meant to leave the temple at five, and nobody was supposed to check on us before then. But even if they did, or if Leto got caught, I don't reckon they could get organised so quickly.'

The way was blocked by a simple STOP sign flanked by two men in slim-fitting blue uniforms and flat peaked caps. Another car was slowing down ahead of us, which gave us a little time.

As if he knew he needed to be as inconspicuous as possible, Argos curled himself up and tucked his head into his paws. I pretended to be asleep too, pulling my hood down to shadow my face.

Aiden's driving licence was requested. The light of a torch swung into the car. 'What are you doing out so late?' one of the men asked.

'My sister was at a party across town and asked me to pick her up,' Aiden replied, copying the man's bored tone.

'Nice dog,' the other one said.

They waved us on.

As soon as we were out of sight, Aiden grimaced. 'They'll remember us, as soon as people start looking for you officially. Argos isn't exactly easy to miss.' He laughed shortly. 'Not only have I seduced a priestess away from the cult, I've kidnapped the High Priestess's dog. Bloody hell.'

I pulled at my lower lip anxiously. 'So what were those men after?'

'Anything or anyone they don't like the look of. Checkpoints are increasingly common these days. After the anarchist bombing campaign in the City, the home secretary pushed through legislation to establish a new Civil Guard. They're basically military police.'

I felt such a child. I'd probably heard a news item about the Civil Guard, and ignored it. I never imagined that this sort of stuff could have anything to do with me.

'A lot of activists will be inspired by your oracle,' Aiden said. 'Especially once they find out how the authorities tried to suppress it. It's obvious Opis and Lionel are running a scam, cooking up false prophecies to fit their own agenda. It's important that people hear it from you.'

Leto had called Aiden my knight in shining armour but this wasn't a romantic rescue. It was a practical one. He needed to recruit me to his cause. And I needed him too, if I was to get my revenge.

Just as the sky began to lighten, Aiden pulled into a large council estate and parked outside a row of shops. He was worried his car could be used to trace us, and so we walked for nearly an hour until we reached a run-down high street not unlike the one where Leto and I had been caught up in the gang battle. Our destination was a boarded-up library. A hole had been cut in the chain-link fence that surrounded the muddy back yard.

Before I ducked through the fence I rummaged in Leto's bag, and pulled out the veil she'd packed me.

'What are you doing?' Aiden asked as I started to pin it over my hair.

'I'm going to be among strangers. I have to cover myself.'

'But,' he said with heavy patience, 'these people are on your side. They'll want to see you. The real you.'

'To gawp at me, you mean.'

'Aura, it's not natural for women – for anyone – to cover their faces. It's repression.'

'Not if it's my choice.'

He made an exasperated sound and went ahead to knock at a small peeling door.

It was a long time before it opened. A white man with dreadlocks squinted through the crack.

'You didn't say nothing about a dog.'

Aiden shrugged an apology. 'He's house-trained.'

'Any trouble along the way?'

'A checkpoint. Couldn't be helped.'

'OK. You'd better come in.'

Argos stuck close to my side, ears pricked, eyes watchful, as we followed our guide into a large basement. The two small windows had been covered with pinned-up cloth, so it was hard to make out the group of people sprawled on cushions on the floor. There was a thick herbal smell that reminded me of the burning laurel leaves, and was combined with body odour and cooking smells. Silence fell as soon as we came through the door.

Aiden cleared his throat. 'Hi, everyone. This is Aura. She's left – escaped – the Cult of Artemis.'

A woman darted forward. She touched her hand to her brow.

'Honoured Lady!'

I shrank back. The title didn't feel like it belonged to me. Not yet.

'I saw you,' she said breathlessly, staring into my eyes. 'In the shopping centre. I was at the foot of the escalator – I heard it all. I felt the goddess's presence . . . all around like . . . like a dark light!'

I didn't know how to respond.

'Afterwards, the men from the Trinovantum Council came, with the Civil Guard, to take my statement,' she gabbled. 'But they didn't listen to me. No. They said I was

121

wrong. They said I was drunk, unreliable. But I knew. I *knew.*'

She did look unreliable. A prematurely creased face, eyes a bit too wide, smile a bit too shaky. Smell of booze on her breath.

'Thank you for believing me,' I said. My voice felt rusty.

The rest of our audience certainly didn't look convinced. They were young, mostly, and I found it hard to distinguish their features among the uniform layers of tattoos, piercings, shapeless clothes and hard stares. Next to them, Aiden, who was still in his suit, looked even more out of place than I did.

A freckle-faced girl got up to pat Argos. 'So are you gonna have another one?' she asked abruptly.

'Another oracle?'

'Yeah.'

'I don't know.'

'But you reckon you can see the future?'

'I . . . suppose. When Holy Artemis wants me to.'

A boy with a spider tattoo on his neck stifled a laugh. Somebody else sniggered.

I looked at Aiden. 'May I go to my room?'

Everything went quiet again. I'd obviously said the wrong thing.

'Sure,' said Aiden awkwardly. 'I'll, um, help you get settled.'

As soon as we left, the place erupted into noisy comment.

There wasn't an actual room. Just a space carved out of the main library with a partition of empty bookshelves and filing cabinets. The mattress on the floor didn't look particularly clean. Argos sniffed around suspiciously. I thought of the priestesses' quarters I was supposed to have moved into this morning. The new bed linen I'd chosen with Cally, three hundred thread count Egyptian cotton . . . But I mustn't think of Cally. Or Artemisia House.

'Do you live in this place?' I asked Aiden, trying not to let my dismay at the squalor show.

'I stay here sometimes. There's a flat – that is, my family has a flat. In the West End. But it wouldn't be safe there.' He frowned. 'For either of us.'

'How long am I going to stay?'

'I don't know.'

'We have to get my true prophecy out. We have to expose Opis.'

'Right.'

But he didn't say anything more. My escape had been so well thought out that I'd imagined Aiden had planned everything else as well. Now I realised that he, too, was improvising.

With Argos stretched out beside me, I curled up on the mattress. I was instantly plunged into a tangle of lurid and fragmented dreams. I woke up with a start, my heart pounding. A tall figure loomed over me.

'It's only me,' said Aiden. 'It's nearly nine, so I thought I'd better wake you. And I got you something to eat.'

He'd changed into fraying jeans and a T-shirt and had brought a kebab and chips, plus a couple of burgers for Argos. 'Sorry it's not very fancy.'

I looked at the change Aiden was jangling in his hand. The small silver and bronze coins meant nothing to me. I'd never handled, let alone owned, actual cash. It struck me with renewed force that I wasn't just a fugitive – I was a charity case. Eating chunks of grease out of a bag on the floor.

Still, by this point I was too hungry to care. I took my example from Argos, who gobbled up his burgers in about three seconds flat.

Aiden had also brought me a newspaper. The front page showed a man in military uniform. General Ferrer was his name, and he'd given a high-profile TV interview, calling for order. He was strong-jawed and broad-shouldered with a bluff, weather-beaten face and a fatherly expression.

I looked up from the paper. 'Ferrer . . . like *ferrum*? The Latin word for iron?'

'It's an old English surname,' said Aiden, helping himself to a chip. 'Means blacksmith.'

'The iron-worker turned Iron Lord.'

'Exactly. The army's seen as heroes by a lot of people. Victims, too, of an unpopular foreign war. The view is that they, like everyone else, have been shafted by the government. General Ferrer is a well-connected guy as well as a war hero. Plays squash with the chancellor, is old university buddies with Lionel Winter . . . And now there are whispers that all leave has been cancelled for the Civil Guard.'

'What does that mean?'

'That the second part of your oracle might be about to come true.' He sighed. 'Look. You said the Iron Lord steals a march and cries havoc, right? Well, "havoc" is an old military order – the signal to start pillaging. "To steal a march" is a military expression too. It means secretly moving your troops around. So your oracle suggests the army is going to make a move. A power-grab, in fact.'

I felt a creeping in the pit of my stomach. 'And Opis and Lionel are in on it.'

Aiden nodded. 'If there is, in fact, a coup, then I reckon the cult will support it. More than that – they'll back it up with some nice supportive oracles. They know that the more frightened people are the more superstitious they get.'

Opis's hissed accusations in the passageway suddenly made sense. She must have thought I'd overheard her and Lionel discussing General Ferrer and his plans. No wonder she'd wanted to shut me up.

'I need to thank you properly,' I said, a little stiffly. 'I suppose it's because I hardly know where to start. If it hadn't been for you, and Leto –'

'Don't worry about it.' He flashed me a quick grin. 'Rescuing a damsel in distress is all in a day's work for us newfangled delinquents.'

'The goddess led you to me.'

'The goddess has nothing to do with it.'

'But you believe –'

'I believe you saw the future. But I don't believe in some moon-lady perched on top of Mount Olympus.'

I frowned. 'I am in the hands of Artemis. I'm her servant. She has a plan for me.'

'You're nobody's servant, Aura. And there is no Divine Plan. After all, Artemis hasn't shot down Opis with an arrow, has she? Or saved all the other girls who were drugged in that crypt?'

There was anger in his voice, yet he looked at me as if he was sorry for me. I couldn't bear his pity. He was giving words to my own secret doubts.

'So the rumours are true,' a voice drawled from the entrance to my cubbyhole. 'Life in the cult really is all sex, drugs and rock 'n' roll.'

It was Scarlet, the rock star's daughter.

'You made it!' Aiden exclaimed, clearly relieved at the interruption.

'Fashionably late, as always.' She sauntered over to shake my hand. 'Well, hello there, Lady Oracle. Welcome to the real world.'

She didn't look particularly real-world herself, in a slinky acid-yellow dress and oversized shades, cigarette drooping from her mouth. It was the kind of outfit that would turn heads wherever she went – she certainly had Aiden's full attention. Surely her presence here was a security risk.

'You're part of the resistance?' I asked doubtfully.

'I tend to leave the manning-the-barricades stuff to Aid. Think of me as your personal media consultant.'

'Scarlet's really well connected,' Aiden put in. 'She's got all sorts of contacts in the press.'

'So you're a journalist?'

'I've appeared in a lot of newspapers,' she said drily. 'Mostly in the gossip columns. Attracting attention is something of a speciality of mine. That's why I'm going to help get you into the spotlight.'

'Thank you,' I said, trying to sound like I meant it.

'Oh, I'm thinking of my CV as well as yours. Let's face it, managing the PR for a runaway priestess is a step up from blogging for crappy online style mags.' She stubbed out her cigarette. 'No offence.'

Then somebody shouted from downstairs.

'What?' I asked, my heart in my mouth. 'What is it?'

Aiden straightened his shoulders. 'It's begun.'

CHAPTER 11

The prime minister, Nicholas Riley, was arrested this morning for the murder of Sir Alan Greendale and charges relating to electoral fraud.

An Emergency Governing Committee, formed by the chancellor, Malcolm Greeve, has ordered the dissolution of Parliament and called for new elections. Greeve is supported by General Sir Charles Ferrer, Chief of the Defence Staff and head of the Armed Forces.

A statement is expected from the committee within the hour.

BBC News

I pinned my veil back over my face and hurried downstairs, joining the other residents around the battered

TV in the basement. It was there we heard the chancellor address the nation, General Ferrer at his side:

'The committee's only concern is the well-being of our country, which has been in a state of upheaval and hardship for so long. Our goal is to hold credible elections in the shortest possible period of time. In the meantime, I request that you remain calm and support us in the re-establishment of order. Together, we will rebuild this great nation . . .'

Not so long ago I would have taken these soothing words at face value. I knew better now. This wasn't the restoration of democracy. It was an outright power-grab.

Malcolm Greeve wasn't nearly as impressive-looking as General Ferrer. He was small and sweaty, with oddly bulging eyes. I'd seen them up close plenty of times, since the chancellor was a regular worshipper at the temple. At the end of Greeve's speech, I spotted an even more obvious link between the coup and cult – Lionel Winter, standing among the other Emergency Committee members in the background.

Over the rest of that long day and night, the rumours flew thick and fast. The cabinet were under house arrest . . . the armour units of the tank division were on standby . . . all TV stations were under the control of the Civil Guard . . . the royal family had fled the country . . .

None of this turned out to be true. The next morning, the BBC aired a live broadcast from the Temple of Artemis. The priestess who had prophesised the murder of Sir Alan Greendale, and the rise of the Iron Lord, was going to be formally introduced to the world.

There on the flickering TV screen were Opis and Cally, standing at the top of the temple steps, flanked by Sebastian and Lionel Winter. Cally was dressed as she had been for her initiation, but unveiled, her eyes demurely lowered for the duration of Opis's announcement.

The Python's Child shall preach with a double tongue.

The meaning seemed obvious now. The goddess warned of an oracle corrupted. Two-faced, dissembling . . .

Opis must have intended to give the pro-coup oracles herself, until my performance in the shopping centre had spoiled her plans and she had to make Cally her mouthpiece instead. There were no signs she was giving up her position as High Priestess, however. And Cally seemed more than happy to play along. She'd clearly got over her fear of divine retribution.

Then, as the speech ended and the party got ready to go into the temple, I saw her turn and look up at Seb. It was only a moment, yet the eagerness in her face made my heart contract.

Back in the television studio, a panel of experts was assembled to give an updated analysis of the oracle. Aiden immediately pressed the mute button on the TV remote. The rest of the audience looked round in surprise.

'Those people don't know what they're talking about,' Aiden said. 'That's why we've got to put Aura out there. She needs to tell her story. The oracle is being used as a propaganda tool.'

'Sorry, but I don't believe either or any of 'em can predict the future,' said the spider-tattoo boy. 'And what does it matter anyway? A load of mumbo-jumbo from the spirit world isn't going to stop tanks rolling down the streets.'

'Churchill consulted the oracle during the war,' an older Asian man said.

'Yeah, and he probably read his horoscope too. So what?'

'But the Honoured Lady's prediction has already come true,' insisted the woman – Sal – from the shopping centre. 'Just like I told you it would.'

'She said it would be the Iron Lord – Ferrer – who took charge. But it's the chancellor who's leading the government, not the general,' somebody pointed out.

'I don't believe that for a moment,' said Aiden impatiently. 'And you can forget all those promises about "credible elections". This Emergency Committee is a front for a military coup. The chancellor is its public face but it'll be General Ferrer who calls the shots. I wouldn't be surprised if it was him who ordered the hit on Sir Alan Greendale – framing the PM for murder was all part of the takeover plan.'

'Exactly,' said the freckle-faced girl. 'And if that bimbo on the telly starts having more chats with Artemis, and Artemis tells her we'd all be better off without democracy and under army rule . . . well, what if people start listening?'

A boy with a greasy quiff nodded. 'My gran, right, she's mostly Church of England. But she keeps this little statue of Artemis on her mantelpiece, next to my grandad's ashes. She always says the goddess comes to her people in their hour of need.'

'Your granny's not the only one,' said Scarlet. She had spent the discussion lounging on a beanbag, picking neon polish off her nails. I hadn't realised she was listening. 'There are literally millions of people like her. The cult will mobilise them. General Ferrer will mobilise them, so that people feel better about him, and themselves.'

Up till now, though I wanted to speak up, I didn't feel I'd earned the right. Everyone else in this squat had been on protests and demonstrations and spent nights in police cells. They'd been in this fight for months – years – longer than I had.

Still, now it was my fight too. I got to my feet. 'Scarlet and Aiden are right. Most people have stopped trusting politicians, but they still trust in the oracle. That makes it a powerful weapon. We can't afford for it to be in the wrong hands.'

Scarlet planned to make a film of me recounting the true prophecy, which would then be uploaded on to the internet. 'We need it to go viral,' she said.

Once again, I felt the full force of my cluelessness. I could compose poetry in ancient Greek and make foie gras canapés, but I had little idea how the internet worked.

I wanted Aiden, not Scarlet, to be the one to explain it to me. When I asked him, the conversation led on to how he knew Scarlet, which was apparently through mutual friends at school.

'So she's your girlfriend?'

He looked surprised. 'No. At least – we used to date. But we're better off as friends.'

I wondered if Scarlet agreed with him. Still, I was embarrassed to have let my curiosity get the better of me. I quickly moved on to another question.

'How's Scarlet involved with the cult?'

'She's not really. It's her dad. He's famous, or used to be. Not that his name will mean anything to you –'

'Rick Moodie,' I said nonchalantly. 'That wrinkly old musician guy. He came to see Opis for a private oracle the other day, then had a massive row about it.'

It had been the same day as my oracle in fact. Whatever Opis told him hadn't been to his liking. The priestesses whispered that he'd turned up drunk and had to be wrestled out of the temple by the guards.

Aiden laughed. 'Yeah, so I heard. He's fairly eccentric and has a bit of a goddess-obsession. He's retired to this wacky mansion somewhere outside London, where he apparently wants to set up his own cult. Anyway, Scarlet isn't like that. She's got her head screwed on. She saw, right from the start, how important you are.'

'For the cause?'

'Of course. You're our prime asset.'

An asset, a weapon, a mouthpiece for a goddess. Artemis had chosen me for this purpose, I told myself. It would be wrong to want anything more.

Like Cally, I was in costume for the film, wearing my initiation dress with the gold clasps and belt. It showed the effects of being bundled under jogging bottoms and a sweatshirt during my getaway. Still, the more authentic I looked, the more compelling my statement would be.

Not everyone agreed that my face should be veiled. There was a concern that our film might inspire copy-cats. But the issue was settled when one of the group's contacts brought word that the Trinovantum Council were already making discreet enquiries as to the where-abouts of a girl of my description. Since handmaidens and priestesses were never photographed barefaced, whoever was looking for me would have to rely on a police artist's sketch. The longer my face stayed hidden, the safer I would be.

The filming was done by the spider-tattoo boy, known as Spidey, on a digital video camera. He called himself a 'hacktivist' and belonged to Alias, an online community of computer nerds turned political protesters.

Scarlet helped Aiden write my script. The other girls in the squat watched her jealously and were always extra-attentive to Aiden when she was around. Me, they mostly ignored. The veil had turned me into a victim in their eyes, someone passive and helpless, without a voice. *I'll show them*, I thought. *I'll show everyone.*

* * *

'My name is Aura, and on my sixteenth birthday I became a priestess in the Cult of Artemis. But on the night of my initiation I had to run away.

'This is because I discovered that an oracle I'd received from the Goddess had been deliberately falsified. To stop me from revealing its true content, the High Priestess locked me up and deprived me of food and water. During my initiation, she tried to pimp me to a member of the Trinovantum Council.

'I am here to tell you that the Cult of Artemis is plotting with the Emergency Committee to turn our country into a military dictatorship and –'

I was no good. I was wooden and stilted and supremely unconvincing.

'Take a deep breath,' said Aiden through gritted teeth, after I stumbled over the intro yet again. Scarlet was 'supervising' from a corner, though she left the directing to Aiden and filming to Spidey. As time wore on, her yawns, sighs and foot-tapping became harder to ignore.

Finally I cracked. She had rolled her eyes once too often.

'Look, I know this goddess-thing sounds crazy, OK?' I snapped at her. 'Until recently, I had no idea what receiving an oracle actually involved. And then Artemis spoke to me – no, it was more than that: *she took me over*. And it was terrifying. The most mind-shreddingly terrifying thing you can imagine.

'I'm not even close to understanding how it happened. Or why she chose me. But I *know* the words I spoke were true – otherwise why would people try to cover them up, to twist them? They're making the goddess tell lies. They're stealing the oracle, and they're stealing this country. That's why you should listen to me.'

I paused for breath. Aiden looked across at Spidey.

'You got that?'

'Every bit.' He lowered the camera. 'Nice work.'

Scarlet gave a complacent smile. 'See? I knew you could do it, Aura. You just needed a little push.'

Spidey was convinced that the authorities were collecting records of activists' text messages and email exchanges, but was confident that he could fix things so that they couldn't track us online. He sent the link to my film to bloggers and campaigners around the world, as well as media outlets and social networking sites. His fellow cyber-guerrillas in Alias helped spread the word. Although the film got little or no coverage on TV and in the main-stream press, it still found an audience. The number of views it collected on a video-sharing website exceeded all our expectations – first hundreds, then thousands, then millions.

'Told you,' said Scarlet. 'Sex sells. Even in the midst of a military takeover, scandal and conspiracy in the Cult of Artemis is hot news.'

Although the internet chat rooms were buzzing, the streets were quiet. The nation seemed to be holding its breath. I could see why most people were desperate to believe the committee's promises that human rights and free speech would be protected, that the corrupt would be brought to justice and the economy revived.

Three days after we posted the film, and when the number of online views hit the twenty million mark, access to the video-sharing website was temporarily blocked, allegedly due to a technical hitch. When it came back, our film was no longer there. Spidey said it didn't matter; there were other places to post it, and it had already spread too far and wide to be suppressed. He must have been right, for the next day, the Cult of Artemis released a press statement. It said that I was a deeply troubled individual, with severe behavioural issues. Every effort was being made to get me the help and support I needed.

This was followed by Cally making guest appearances on *This Morning*, BBC *Breakfast* and *Newsnight*.

'She's good,' said Aiden. 'But a little too practised, don't you think? A bit *too* perfect. You, on the other hand, came across as much more real. Raw.'

'That's the trouble,' I said gloomily. 'They're saying I'm deranged. They even made a big deal about me kidnapping poor Argos. Why would anyone believe me over Cally?'

Aiden shook his head. 'A girl like Callisto belongs in a different time – back when things were shiny and certain, and everybody had something to sell. I'm not so sure the public will warm to her.'

I wished I could believe him. Still, we made and posted another film in response, in which Aiden – his face and voice digitally disguised – described his involvement in my initiation, and how the Trinovantum Council was involved in political corruption, sexual exploitation and fraud.

Watching it made me queasy. This wasn't just because of the emotions stirred up by revisiting my initiation night. I didn't know how much longer I could stand washing in cold water, sleeping on a stained mattress and having to share my living space with strangers.

The Emergency Committee had imposed a curfew at night and it wasn't safe for most people to leave the building during the day. I worried for Argos, unable to exercise anywhere but the muddy back yard. I was anxious about Leto, and whether Opis would suspect her of helping me. I was homesick for Artemisia House and missed the other girls. Even Cally. But I couldn't think of them without thinking of my mother, and I was afraid of where that might lead.

I no longer wondered if I would have another oracle. It was only a question of when. I was discovering the difference between ordinary anxiety and the shadow the goddess had cast. I could sense her at all times, like the breath of something on my skin. Something ancient and ageless, inhuman.

The only person with whom I could let my guard down was Aiden. He was also the only person for whom I'd unveil myself, since he'd already seen me barefaced. Plus he complained that talking to me with a veil was like trying to make conversation with a curtain.

It was certainly more intimate, face to face. It was also unsettling. He had a way of looking at me sometimes that was especially concentrated, as if he was reading my innermost emotions. As if he could tell when I was thinking about him.

My idea of male good looks came from the mosaics

in the temple, or the classical art I'd studied. Aiden, with his ranginess and his restlessness, his bitten-down fingernails and untamed hair, didn't fit this aesthetic. But I was seeing a lot of things differently these days.

At night, he slept outside the entrance to my make-shift room. Sometimes I could hear him mumbling in his sleep and once I heard him cry out. I got up to check he was all right. Under a patch of moonlight, I could see the blanket had been pushed back; he was sleeping on his stomach wearing just his shorts. I was worried he might get cold and reached to pull up the blanket. His naked back was long and brown. I thought how smooth it would be to touch.

Then I looked back to my own mattress and saw Argos was awake, panting gently. His eyes glinted. I under-stood, then, that the goddess was watching too. *Remember who you are.*

On Friday morning, a new arrival called Tiggs went out on an errand that was only supposed to take half an hour and didn't come back. Nor did she answer her phone. As time wore on, anxiety in the squat increased. Tiggs was wanted by the police for questioning after taking part in a protest inside a bank. We'd heard that arrests and raids were going on in secret. Scarlet was keeping away, and hadn't visited for days.

At six o'clock, a meeting was held in the basement to debate how worried we should or shouldn't be. I didn't go. Instead, I retreated to my mattress, staring at the dust-furred bookshelves from under a pile of blankets. The library would have been a draughty place at the best of times, with its high ceilings and large windows. Now that the windows were broken and inadequately boarded up, the place was freezing. Damp too – for the roof had several leaks.

There was a collection of dirty pots and pans on the floor to catch the drips. Every *tip-tap* of water made me wince. Argos was as restless as I was. He began to whine, and I saw that his fur was all standing on end. Then I myself began to bristle all over with a strange and sickly energy. The air hummed.

Somehow I managed to stumble down to the basement.

'Aiden –' I gasped, doubled over in the doorway.

'Is she ill?' someone asked. People were getting up and gathering around me, too loud and too close. I couldn't breathe.

'Give the Honoured Lady space!' Sal cried. 'It's the goddess in her – the dark light!'

Yes, I thought confusedly, as I thrashed about. A *dark light . . . that's what it's like.*

'Aiden! She's coming. Help me –'

I felt him push the others away, then his hands were on mine. The world was a whirling, rushing darkness, until I fixed my eyes on his and found gravity again.

I howled, and Argos howled with me. All the light went out.

I was buried in darkness, the weight of stone pressing above and around me. I was in the crypt. I was in my tomb. I was in a cave.

Beware –

I crawled across jagged rock. The darkness glimmered and the cave mouth gaped. Spread out before me was a vast grey waste. There has never been anything so empty or so desolate.

I stood on the mountains of the moon, my mouth full of ashes, as infinite night poured through my eyes.

Beware –

'Beware the shepherd of the Hot Gates. For the archers are drawing back their bows, and their feet will soon be on the Anopaea Path. Beware –'

* * *

I jerked about violently, but this time I didn't black out, or only for a moment. Several of the people gathered around me were holding up their camera phones.

'Jesus Christ,' said one of them.

'Artemis Selene,' someone else corrected him.

Other voices chimed in.

'What *was* that?'

'What do you think? The priestess had another oracle!'

'No, she had a fit.'

'So you're deaf as well as blind?'

'But what does it *mean*?'

'It means we've got to get out of here,' said Aiden.

More questions were flung from every side. I was too dazed to respond. Argos was at my side and licked my hand, tail wagging cheerfully.

'Let the Lord Herne speak!' Sal cried, cutting through the noise.

Aiden looked uncomfortable but spoke up all the same. 'Aura's prophecy referenced the Battle of Thermopylae. And the local man, I can't remember his name, who showed the invading Persian army – that's the archers – a secret path around the pass, so they could attack the Greeks.' He gave me a lopsided smile. 'You're not the only one with a Classical education, you know.'

'Ephialtes,' I whispered. 'The traitor's name was Ephialtes.'

'All right, but why does this mean we have to leave?' someone asked impatiently.

'It means that Tiggs has got into trouble and told the authorities where to find us,' Aiden replied. 'The police or Civil Guard are probably already on their way.'

There was a babble of protest and alarm. The group had an evacuation plan for just this kind of emergency, but while some people immediately rushed off to collect their things, others huddled together, still arguing.

Aiden took me by the arm. 'Don't worry, Scarlet and her dad will give us a place to stay. It's high time we got you out of London anyway.'

'This is where all the action is,' I objected. 'Don't we need to be in the centre of things?'

'It's too dangerous.'

'But how can we even leave the city? Aren't there checkpoints on all the roads and at every train station?'

'Honoured Lady,' Sal whispered. She plucked at my sleeve with shaking hands. 'If you and the Lord Herne come with me, I have a friend who might be able to help.'

CHAPTER 12

The search continues for a young woman with mental problems who has gone missing from the Cult of Artemis. It is feared that she has fallen into the hands of insurgents, who are setting her up as a puppet oracle to promote their extremist agenda. A substantial reward is offered for her safe return.

Citizens are advised that publicising the impostor's claims is now a criminal offence.

BBC News

There was no time to say more than a hurried goodbye. I had to trust that Artemis had given all of us enough time to flee. Aiden, Sal, the dog and I squeezed out through the wire fence and into a rain-soaked early evening. It helped that it was the pre-curfew rush hour and the streets were busy. I did my best to conceal my face with my hooded top and a scarf. Argos stuck to the shadows of his own accord.

Just as we turned a corner a few streets away from the library, Aiden abruptly drew me and Sal into the doorway of a crowded supermarket. Two unmarked black vans were speeding down the road. 'Those belong to the private security firm used by the Trinovantum Council,' he said. 'We got out just in time.'

I looked round for Argos but the dog had vanished. I couldn't call him because it would draw too much attention.

'Maybe it's for the best,' Aiden said. 'He's a smart animal. He's probably just headed home.'

I continued to scan the street, eyes blurry with tears, the aftershock of the oracle still thrumming through my body. I knew the goddess would protect Argos, but I felt abandoned all the same. The wolfhound was my last link to my old life. I couldn't even risk the shelter of a veil any more.

We didn't dare take public transport or even Aiden's car, so it was fortunate Sal's friend didn't live far, in a dilapidated tower block. The lift was broken and we were all breathless by the time we climbed five flights of stairs in a dank stairwell. The door to Flat 203 was opened by a fat middle-aged lady with a frizz of badly dyed red hair.

'My,' she said when she saw me, 'you're just a wisp of a thing! Not like that other girl on the telly. Still, I suppose Blessed Artemis knows what she's doing.'

Her tiny living room was a shrine to the goddess, stuffed with statues, prayer beads and prints I recognised from the temple gift shop. Floral incense sticks failed to conceal a strong smell of cat.

We drank cups of stewed tea, while Sal's friend – Mrs Galloway – explained the security situation. As we'd feared, there were checkpoints operating on all roads out of London and police patrols in the train stations. 'The official line is that they're looking for terrorists,' said our host. 'Chances are, they won't want to make the hunt for you public, in case it gives your story more cred.'

I wondered how she knew all this, and how she knew Sal. Sal had said they went to the same book group, but I didn't see any books in the flat. Mrs Galloway certainly seemed well connected; she said her contacts would be able to get us out of the city undetected, no problem. Meanwhile, Aiden was busy texting Scarlet on his phone – a cheap, disposable model that couldn't be traced.

After tea, the two ladies went off to 'set things up'. Looking for the toilet, I opened a door to a small room bursting with random stuff: antique candlesticks, electronic equipment, a mink coat . . . even a mini-fridge.

'What's all this?' I asked Aiden. 'There's enough here to open a shop.'

'I'd say Mrs G is a fence.'

'A what?'

'Someone who takes in stolen goods. Cheer up – she can't be any more of a crook than the lot you ran away from.'

The next moment, Mrs Galloway and Sal returned, looking very pleased with themselves. Mrs Galloway explained that her nephew worked in the local freight yard. All the trains there were for the transportation of goods, not passengers, and so weren't subject to the same security checks. We could hitch a ride on one out of the city.

The first challenge was getting us to the freight yard now that curfew was in force. This was what Mrs Galloway and Sal had gone to 'set up'. Five minutes after their return, there was a knock on the door, and two men pressed into the already crowded sitting room.

'Meet the staff of Elite Cleaning,' said Mrs Galloway.

I looked at them doubtfully. One was shaven-headed and hulking, the other was short and squat and beady-eyed.

'They've got a pass for the curfew,' she said proudly. 'Essential service, cleaners. They'll see you right.'

I tried to thank our host but she'd have none of it. Instead, she got me to sign the backs of a clutch of High Priestess dolls. 'One for me, and the rest for my pension fund.'

Sal kissed my hand on parting. 'Honoured Lady,' she said reverently. 'My whole life, I've wanted to be a part of something – something bigger and better than me. Now I'm part of your story.' Her eyes glistened. 'Nobody can take that away from me.'

The back of Elite Cleaning's van was stuffed with cleaning products and kit. These were moved to one side to reveal the hidden compartment in the bottom of the van. Presumably this was where all those antique candlesticks and laptops were transported.

'Good job you're such a skinny little oracle,' said the hulk, as I squeezed myself in, holding my bag to my chest. Aiden and the other man sat in the back, both in cleaners' uniform, caps pulled low.

It was cramped and stuffy in the sealed compartment. Every time we stopped at traffic lights I seized up with panic, convinced we'd been discovered. We ran into a checkpoint at one point, and I could hear the van doors being opened, and a discussion of paperwork and passes. But whatever the guards saw must have satisfied them, because soon we were on the move again. Ten minutes later we were at the freight yard.

The place was a desolate tangle of oily black tracks and grimy cargo trains. Their clattering and grinding sounded eerie in the dark. It was cold and wet, and the wind was flinging little handfuls of rain in our faces, as Aiden and I waited in the shadows for our guide. Mrs Galloway's nephew didn't look especially pleased to meet us, though he produced a grubby timetable and informed us that the most suitable train would be arriving in an hour. He would come and fetch us when it was time to go.

So we settled down to wait, crouched among rusting containers and other rubbish on the embankment. Members of the yard crew milled about on the other side of the tracks, fluorescent jackets and tired faces shining under the lights.

After about twenty minutes our guide reappeared. He was out of breath and even more grim-faced than before. He'd just got word that the Transport Police were on their way. 'They got a tip-off about thieving on the network. You need to get the hell out of this yard.'

But we had nowhere to go. We stared at each other blankly. Below the embankment, a goods train clanked slowly into life.

'Where's that headed?' Aiden asked.

'Swansea. But –'

'It'll do.' He turned to me. 'Ready?'

I wasn't, but I still ran after him down the bank and towards the track. In spite of myself, I felt a spark of excitement as I heard the man behind us shout and swear.

Up close, the train appeared to be moving much faster. We stumbled alongside it as possible handholds rushed by. Sirens wailed from the other side of the yard; I thought I could hear shouting too. Aiden managed to get a grip on the frame of a goods van; grabbing me by the hand, he leaped upwards on to the ledge by the door, dragging me after him. The train seemed to shriek as it gathered speed.

For a moment, my feet swung above the track, as I clutched at the frame and at Aiden as he scrabbled to open the sliding door. My hands were slippery with sweat. Dirty air roared in our faces. Our bones seemed to rattle with the motion. And then Aiden flung himself inside, and I was there too, lying beside him and breathing hard.

*   *   *

Perhaps it was a sign of the times that the goods van was only half full. We propped ourselves up against sacks of fertiliser and got our breath back. I was shaking all over, but more from excitement than fear. So was Aiden. We looked at each other, and began to laugh, giggling like small children. It was almost as liberating as our crazy train jump.

'I don't know if those police were even looking for us,' Aiden said after we'd calmed down. 'But we should try and get off before the train heads into a station, just in case.'

'OK.' It was hard to think ahead. Now the thrill of our getaway had subsided, I was worrying about Leto and Argos again.

'Getting out of London could work to our advantage,' Aiden continued. 'We've been too constrained in the safe house. With Scarlet's help, we'll have access to a much wider range of resources. If we're going to make you a figurehead for the opposition, we need to move on from the fuzzy recordings and the amateur interviews. Go mainstream.' When I didn't respond, he added, 'I know it's a lot to take in and I'm sorry – I wish it didn't have to be this way.'

'There's nothing to be sorry for,' I said. 'I want to stop these people as much as you do.'

'And I'm really grateful. We all are. It's just . . . well, Britain is a secular country. Religion and politics shouldn't mix.'

'So why are you helping ensure that they do?'

'I have to be practical. You said yourself that the oracle's a weapon in the propaganda war. At the moment, opposition to the coup is weak and disorganised. People need something to rally around.'

'Like a flag. Or a slogan T-shirt.' It came out more curtly than I intended.

'You're worth more to me than just politics, Aura. You know that, don't you?' I sensed, rather than saw, his smile. 'From the first moment we met, you've surprised me. I like that.'

I didn't know how to respond. Was he teasing me again? I decided to tease him back: 'Sal called you the Lord Herne.'

'I'm not Lord anything.' This time, his voice had the edge of irritation. 'And shoehorning Herne the Hunter into the cult has always been a bit of a joke. Since when did Celtic woodland gods hang out with ancient Greek goddesses?'

'At Delphi, the Pythia had a Priest of Apollo to interpret her prophecies –'

'I'm *definitely* not a priest.'

'I'm glad you're with me, though,' I said after a pause. 'I'm glad you're my . . . witness. It would be too much to bear if I was alone.'

He reached for my hand. 'You're not.'

I felt my cheeks grow warm in the dark. Of course he'd touched me before; we'd held hands, too, when the goddess possessed me. But this was different. I was remembering how we'd clung on to the ledge of the train, the length of his body crushed against mine. I moved away. I must be careful. I was a priestess, after all. I'd made my vows.

Time passed. After a while, I saw that Aiden had got out his phone and was using its light to read the timetable Mrs Galloway's nephew had given us. 'We'll be getting to a station before long,' he told me. 'So the next time the train slows down, we need to be ready to jump.'

We slid the door open a crack. So much had happened since the oracle telling us to flee, yet it was only just past midnight. A muddy bank rushed alongside us; the blurred tracks flowed underneath. Our progress seemed relentless. But just as I began to think we were trapped the train approached a point where the tracks diverged. The signal was red.

The train began to slow. I slid the door fully open and crouched on the ledge below. I was afraid of the tracks still sliding under me. I wondered if the rails were electrified. I might fall on to them, or under the wheels, and be crushed. I *can do this*, I told myself. I *can do anything. Artemis is with me.* We seemed to have paused, rather than actually come to a stop, but I couldn't hesitate any longer. I jumped, landing clumsily on gravel near to the tracks. Aiden followed. With a wheeze and a clank, the train moved on.

When we got to the top of the scrubby bank, we could see the outskirts of a town only a short distance ahead, its streets broken down to dreary bungalows and the giant sheds of abandoned superstores. Most of the places I'd visited in Britain were like the Sanctuary: picturesque, with grand proportions and olde worlde styles. Since leaving the cult, I'd seen another kind of country, a country that was ugly and tired and cheaply made.

The trouble was, although we'd escaped London, we'd got out on the wrong side.

'Scarlet didn't manage to leave the city before curfew so won't get to her dad's till morning,' Aiden announced, tapping away at his phone. 'I'll text her to say we'll try and hitchhike part of the way.'

My eyes widened. 'Won't that be dangerous?'

He laughed. 'I keep forgetting you've spent your life being chauffeured around in limos. No, hitchhiking's pretty mainstream these days, especially since petrol prices got so high. And even if we did feel able to risk public transport, there's nothing running at this time of night.'

First, we stopped at a twenty-four-hour supermarket and petrol station just off the motorway. The place had several security guards as well as CCTV, and *Shoplifters Will Be Prosecuted* signs were plastered all over the windows. As I waited outside for Aiden, I watched a heavily pregnant woman get out of a car and carefully count out a small handful of change. Three or four skinny children pressed tired faces against the window of her battered car. *These are your people*, I said to Artemis. *Give them your protection. Have mercy on us all.*

I met Aiden at the back of the petrol station. Furtively, he handed me the make-up he'd bought, and I slipped inside the toilet. The place stank. In the mirror, my tired face looked drained of all colour. White hair, white skin, eyes like glass . . . I didn't know if I looked like a priestess, but I definitely looked like a fugitive.

I used a heavy foundation and bronzer on my face, and eye make-up to darken my brows and eyelashes, scraping back my hair into a high ponytail. It wasn't much of a disguise, but I hoped it would reduce my resemblance to any 'wanted' images that might be in circulation. After a moment's hesitation, I took a folded jumper from my bag and pushed it under my hoody, using the gold priestess belt to fix it round my waist. I'd got the idea from the woman outside the supermarket.

It was hard to keep a straight face when I saw Aiden's expression. The extent of his own disguise was a woolly hat and an up-turned collar. 'They're looking for a mentally ill priestess and her partner in crime,' I said, more breezily than I felt. 'Not a pregnant teen and her boyfriend.'

'Sneaky,' he said. 'And clever. I like it.'

I tried not to look too obviously pleased.

'But you've smudged your mascara,' he added. 'Hold still a sec.'

He leaned in towards me and brushed his thumb under the corner of my right eye. His touch was very gentle, but my whole cheek tingled. Our eyes met. With effort, I moved away.

We walked towards the slip road, and a grassy verge near where the traffic slowed. Lorries thundered past and the wind blew grit into our eyes. I was worried there wouldn't be much traffic at this time of night. But after only twenty minutes, a beaten-up car screeched to a halt a little way down from where we were standing with our thumbs out. The horn tooted.

Aiden took my hand and this time I let him. We had to look like a couple, I told myself, as the driver stuck his fat mottled face out of the window and bellowed 'Roll up! Roll up! Baby on-board!'

While I slid into the back seat, Aiden sat in front and made small talk. 'Yeah, I'm starting work in the morning,' he explained to our new friend, Terry. 'Or I hope so, anyhow. I've got a mate in construction who says he might have something for me.'

'Never thought I'd see the day when a well-spoken lad like you had to thumb his way round the country for a job.'

I tensed. Of course Aiden's voice betrayed his background.

However, his answer was relaxed. 'Me neither. But things are tough for everyone.'

'Too true.' Terry eyed me in the mirror. 'It's a hard world to bring a kid into – and you're hardly more than kids yourselves. Ah well. Maybe the new government will set things right. It's about time this country found its backbone.'

After a while, he put on the radio. A string of mindless pop jingles was followed by the news. The final item was about the search for the missing priestess from the Cult of Artemis.

As the newsreader proceeded to describe me and Aiden, I couldn't breathe. But Terry merely chuckled.

'Sounds to me like there's been a catfight in the cult. There'll be more to this business than meets the eye.'

'I heard they nearly caught the girl yesterday, but she got a tip-off from the goddess and escaped,' said Aiden.

'How about it, love?' Terry glanced at me in the mirror again. 'Which of the two oracles gets your vote? The bimbo or the lunatic?'

CHAPTER 13

The Civil Guard, under the command of General
Ferrer, has raided addresses across the capital as part of
a crackdown on anarchist groups. Up to a hundred
people have been taken into custody on suspicion of
conspiracy to commit acts of terrorism.

In response to the increasing terrorist threat, the
Emergency Committee has announced the creation of
a new State Security Agency and the introduction of
compulsory ID cards for all citizens.

BBC News

Dawn was just breaking as we arrived in the small market
town where Scarlet had arranged to pick us up. We'd
hitched two more lifts after Terry's. The other drivers we
met were anxious and unsettled by recent events, but

seemed resigned. 'Nothing we can do about it,' was the standard response. I was afraid we'd run into another checkpoint, but for now they were only set up in trouble spots and major cities.

There was nothing covert about Scarlet's arrival. She roared up in a red sports car, music pumping from the stereo, her dark glasses the only attempt at camouflage.

'Golly, darling,' she said to Aiden, after kissing him on both cheeks. 'You do pong.'

Then she looked at my bump. 'Congratulations. I see you've made the most of escaping the nunnery.'

I blushed and mumbled something about the need for disguise. Scarlet laughed uproariously, and I felt even more at a disadvantage. I probably smelled too. I was newly conscious of the cheap make-up smudged around my face.

We weren't in the car for long, but it still gave me plenty of time to worry about what kind of impression I'd make on Rick Moodie: rock star, revolutionary and, apparently, Artemis's Number One Fan. Soon we were driving through a wood and on to a wide tree-lined drive that swept up to a sprawling mansion. It wasn't the stately pile I'd been expecting, but a starkly modernist construction of curved glass panels and blinding white walls.

Scarlet parked the car at a rakish angle and hopped out. 'Welcome to the madhouse.'

She led the way into the entrance hall, a glass atrium with a black marble floor. There were sliding doors at the end, leading outside to a paved terrace and a swimming pool. Someone was swimming in it with long, slow strokes. Heat rose from the water and steamed gently in the morning air.

As we stood out on the terrace, the swimmer, a thin blonde woman, swam to the steps and pulled herself out of the water. I looked away in confusion, for she was completely naked.

'Hi, Crystal,' said Scarlet. 'Where's Dad?'

'Who cares?' the dripping woman replied indifferently. She took a glug from the bottle of vodka on the side of the pool and returned to her swim.

Scarlet muttered something under her breath and went back into the house. 'You'd better wait here while I track him down.'

'Actually, do you have a secure telephone line I could use?' Aiden asked. 'I'd like to try and check on the others from the safe house.'

Scarlet told him to come with her. Though I didn't want Aiden to leave me, I was too proud to cling on and so stayed behind in the atrium. There were elliptical stairs on either side, with mirrored steps that seemed to float upwards. Although music wailed and thumped through the walls, there were no other signs of life apart from the woman in the pool. The place felt too bright, too empty. It wasn't long before I decided to follow the others after all. I opened the door I thought they'd gone through, and found a lift. The only option was down.

The lift was mirrored too. When the doors opened, I found myself in a basement corridor. The walls were lined with framed concert posters and record sleeves. At least it was quiet here. I looked into a chrome and black leather cocktail bar; it was littered with dirty glasses and bottles, but otherwise empty. The next door opened to an entertainment suite.

A wide aisle ran between rows of plush seats and slanted down to small stage. I supposed there would be a cinema screen behind the black velvet curtains. Small lights set into the floor glowed softly and built-in speakers hummed from the walls. The sound was faint and murmuring; like the sea, perhaps, or wind in trees.

I was about to turn back when the curtains began to part. They drew back to reveal the goddess.

I caught my breath. Just for a moment, I thought it was really her. Then I realised it was a life-sized replica of the statue in the temple. Bow drawn, hair flowing, hound at her side. The screen behind the statue showed a film of sun-parched mountains and cypress trees.

'Ain't she a babe?'

A little man had emerged from behind the curtains, and gave the statue's behind a pat. 'Real craftsmanship, that,' he said proudly. 'No expense spared.'

'It's, um, remarkable,' I managed to say. 'I'm sorry if I disturbed you. I'm here because . . . well, because I'm –'

'I know who you are, ducky.' He kissed my hand with a nod and a wink. 'Welcome to me humble abode, Honoured Lady.'

The rock star was wearing the same sort of clothes as his daughter: tight ripped jeans, a studded T-shirt. His hair was black and shaggy too. But there the resemblance ended. Rick Moodie was tiny and wizened, with a yellowish face and a goblin grin.

'This is just a temporary arrangement,' he explained, waving his wrinkly hands. 'The plan is to build a proper temple, like the one in London but bigger 'n' better. Artemis will like it here. *You'll* like it here. You'll give more oracles – buckets of 'em. It's the country air, you see. It's holy. Purified.'

I nodded politely, and he lowered his voice to a confiding whisper. 'I've talked with the goddess meself, you know. I had an overdose once, and she came to me in a vision. Queen of the freakin' Beasts. She saved me for me music – that's what people don't understand. Like that High Bitch from your old cult. But you understand. You've been chosen by her, just like me.'

'There you are, Dad,' said Scarlet from the door. 'Crystal's been asking for you.' Then, when he didn't move, 'She's knocking back vodka for breakfast again.'

Rick Moodie reluctantly left the room, though not without blowing me a goodbye kiss. Scarlet lounged on one of the velvet seats and lit up a cigarette. 'I thought an intervention was in order.'

I cast around for something polite to say. 'Your father is very . . . enthusiastic.'

'Nah, he's just nuts.' Her tone was indulgent, a parent humouring a wayward child. 'At least his goddess fetish keeps him out of trouble.'

'That might change if I'm here.'

She eyed me through the smoke. 'You don't think the army's going to storm the place just to drag you home?'

'No.' I said it with more confidence than I felt. 'I've always been free to leave the cult. Its leaders would like to shut me up, that's all.'

'Well, Dad can help with that. He's got the contacts

and the cash to make you mainstream. Or a lot harder to shut up anyway.'

'That's what Aiden says.'

'You like him, don't you?'

She was watching me closely. That was because *she* liked him, I realised. I could – should – have put her mind at rest. But somehow I didn't feel the need.

'I'm very grateful to Aiden,' I said blandly. 'We seem to have a natural connection.'

'That's because he's always been the bleeding-heart, save-the-world type. So congrats on becoming his latest project.' She took another drag of her cigarette. 'You know, I'm totally in awe of you priestess types. A hundred per cent pure in thought, word and deed! It must take super-human levels of self-control.'

I had a flashback to a midnight awakening: Aiden's sleeping murmurs, his naked back in the moonlight. 'Not really.'

The screen behind the statue kept changing. We'd moved from mountains to a ruined temple to a sunlit wood. The bright leaves and dark shadows reminded me of Titian's painting of Actaeon, and not in a good way.

Scarlet must have seen my expression change. 'Seriously,' she said, 'if it was me, I'd go *mad*.'

CHAPTER 14

The Cult of Artemis has been favoured with a second oracle, predicting a new age of peace and prosperity. Witnesses described the priestess responsible as 'serene and radiant'. The leader of the Emergency Committee, Malcolm Greeve, will receive a private oracle from her later this week.

The cult plans to honour his visit by sponsoring a chain of inner-city food banks. Food prices rose to a record high last month but, says a cult spokesperson, 'Artemis will provide.'

BBC News

I was given an enormous room decorated with metallic paint and studded leather. The bed was not much smaller than the swimming pool and I fell upon it with a little sob of relief.

I slept deeply and undisturbed for the first time since leaving the cult. Perhaps this was why I dreamed of the initiation night. The nightmare seemed to go on for hours, a labyrinth of dark passageways and flickering braziers, in which shadowy figures pursued me through smoke. I woke up in a sweat to find it was two in the afternoon.

I felt better after a shower. The cupboard was full of clothes that Scarlet said had been left by a groupie, and I helped myself to an ankle-length black kaftan. I tied my hair back with a purple fringed scarf as a compromise veil. From the window, I looked over the front drive and surrounding wood. It was hard to believe we were only an hour's drive outside London. The house felt entirely shut off from the world. This should have reassured me, but I'd lost my faith in so-called sanctuaries.

I found Aiden and Scarlet by the pool. The bad weather of the past weeks had given way to a fine June afternoon, and Scarlet was resplendent in a microscopic lime bikini. The two of them were leaning intently over a laptop. It was all very cosy.

'Good nap?' asked Scarlet, not looking entirely pleased by the interruption.

Aiden gave me a quick smile. 'You're an internet hit again. There's mobile-phone footage of you giving the warning about the police raid on the squat. Spidey got out in time and has been spreading the word. And people are demonstrating outside the Houses of Parliament, calling for elections. A protest camp has been set up in the square.'

He and Scarlet were determined to make the most of my new-found celebrity and had set up a meeting that evening with Rick Moodie's agent and an American journalist called Lindy Ryan.

I supposed it was my fault for sleeping so long, but I wished I'd been consulted. While I felt indebted to Scarlet and her father, who were taking a big risk on my behalf, the house's other inmates didn't exactly inspire confidence. Crystal (Rick's girlfriend – Scarlet's mother lived in LA) floated about in various states of undress, face blank and eyes glazed. She had a friend called Seraphina, who went in for tie-die drapes and a great deal of bangles. Whenever she saw me, Seraphina would press her hands together with the greeting 'Namaste, Guru' and a beatific smile.

I still preferred this to Rick Moodie's pestering. 'Can you feel her yet?' he kept asking. 'Is she coming?'

It was what everyone was waiting for, including myself. I was aware of the goddess's closeness at all times, as a kind of shadow and shine in the corner of my eyes. In the meantime, I wandered restlessly around the house. In the midst of its sharp angles and blank walls, the lights glaring through glass, I felt like a fly buzzing against a window.

The house, though, was the reason for Lindy Ryan's visit. It had been going to feature on a US life-and-style TV show that she presented, as part of a series showcasing the homes of celebrities. She had been ready to cancel after the coup, until Rick Moodie persuaded her to interview me instead.

Most of the household staff had been sent away, so catering for the dinner party fell to Crystal. We helped ourselves from bowls of goji berries, platters of smoked salmon and tins of caviar. And drink. Lots of it. The dining room was the only source of colour in the house, its walls covered in glossy purple tiles, with a black mirrored table in the centre. It was the kind of place you could imagine a serial killer eating his dinner.

Lindy dominated the conversation. She was a woman of uncertain age, with a pillowy pink pout and waves of frosted blonde hair. Swapping a celebrity lifestyle feature for an exclusive with Britain's runaway oracle was quite a scoop, and she had arranged for our interview to be broadcast on her network's lunchtime chat show. Thanks to Spidey, it would also be live-streamed on the internet channel that had been set up by Alias hacktivists for anti-Emergency Committee broadcasts.

'Of course,' said Lindy, 'we have a ton of cults and doomsday prophets back home. But there's just something so darn classy about the ancient Greeks. And you Brits, of course . . . Hey, you know what would be great? If Aura could give an oracle during the broadcast. The viewers would go *nuts*.'

'Too right. In fact, if things don't work out over here, you should consider a move across the pond,' Rick's agent, Noah Evans, told me. He was a thin streak of a man with slicked-back hair and too many teeth. 'With good representation, you might go far.'

'Aura's not a novelty act,' said Aiden.

Noah grinned at him humourlessly. 'Don't worry, kid. You'll still get your cut.'

'The oracle's staying *here*,' Rick insisted, thumping the table so hard the plates clattered. 'This is her sanctuary. This is her *destiny*.'

'Whatever her destiny, she needs a change of image,' said Scarlet, examining her own reflection in the back of a spoon. 'Pagan doesn't have to mean frumpy.'

'Body glitter!' exclaimed Crystal, briefly roused from her stupor. Seraphina clapped her hands in glee.

Voices got louder, faces redder, gestures more expansive. Cigarette smoke lay over the table in an eye-watering cloud. I had to slip into the study next door before I was tempted to scream or throw something. A minute or so later I heard voices in the corridor.

'Giving Aura a makeover is hardly a priority,' said Aiden's voice.

Scarlet gave her throaty laugh. 'Don't tell me you find her nun-on-the-run look a turn-on.'

'It's got nothing to do with –'

'I suppose it's only to be expected. You never could resist a lost soul.'

'And you never used to be so catty.'

'Are you sure? It's been a while, darling. Maybe you've just remembered me wrong.'

'Scarlet . . .'

There was silence. Had he moved towards her, or away? I felt light-headed, imagining the scene. I couldn't bear to listen any more. There were doors at the end of the study, and I went into the atrium. It was especially disorientating at night. The lights inside and the darkness outside were both reflected in the marble floor and mirrored steps, the huge glass panes.

I saw Aiden reflected in one of them and turned

round. His eyes were narrow and green, his expression shadowed, and he rubbed his hands through his hair. The gesture was familiar; so was his exasperation. My chest ached.

'How can these people help us?' I cried. 'Body glitter! Chat shows! Nothing's serious to them. Nothing's *real*.'

'You'll make it real when you talk tomorrow.'

'Are you in love with her?'

He stared. 'What?'

'You and Scarlet. Are you getting back together? Is that why she's helping you?'

'She's helping me – us – because she believes in our cause. Yes, we were together for a while, I told you that, but it didn't work out and we stayed friends. Hey . . . what's this?' My eyes were glistening. Angrily, I struck the tears away, and he touched my cheek. My whole body hummed.

'Forget I said anything. I shouldn't have asked.'

'You have the right.' He took a step closer to me. His voice was very soft. 'You have the right to ask me anything.'

'No, I don't. You and Scarlet . . . I shouldn't care. I'm not allowed to. I'm a priestess. I . . . I've made vows.'

It was the first time I'd spoken of my vows. Since Aiden was well aware of what they involved, I knew that making even the slightest reference to them was an admission. I'd as good as confessed to being tempted. By him.

Aiden frowned. He'd lost weight over the last week, and the angles of his face looked sharper. He looked impossibly adult. And, suddenly, impossibly distant. 'Your vows were made to a corrupt authority. You can't be held to them.'

'I made them to the goddess,' I whispered. 'I have to be pure for her.'

'Even if it will make you unhappy? Even though it will keep you alone?'

'Why should we think the gods are any better than us? I told you they made us in their own image. Jealous, fickle, cruel.'

'Aura.' He reached for my hand. 'Listen to me –'

I wrenched myself free. 'I don't want to talk about this any more.' The violence of my words startled us both. 'Please, just leave me alone.'

I went out and stood by the swimming pool, breathing in the night air.

The moon's cold eye was veiled by cloud, but I felt her

gaze just the same. I could hear the wind in the trees, a dog barking. The pool was covered in a clear sheet. I imagined stepping out on to it, the cover cracking like ice as I sank slowly into depths of warm blue.

CHAPTER 15

It has been confirmed that a special tribunal will conduct the trial of the prime minister, Nicholas Riley, for the assassination of Sir Alan Greendale. Riley denies all charges and has denounced the tribunal as a 'show-trial and farce'.

BBC News

Filming started the next evening at eight. First, though, I had my makeover. It emerged that Crystal had been a make-up artist in another life; surrounded by the tools of her trade she became a different woman, capable and quick.

The body glitter she'd talked about at dinner was actually a discreet silver shimmer. My eyes were outlined in black kohl, my hair styled in soft waves. I wore a clinging indigo silk dress. When I looked in the mirror, I had undergone a metamorphosis. I saw a stranger: elegant, chilly, glittering. But this costuming was different from the lipsticks and party frocks I'd bought with the credit marks from my allowance in the cult. I wasn't a little girl playing dressing-up any more. This had to be real.

'Told you, didn't I?' said Scarlet with lazy satisfaction. 'Now you're a force to be reckoned with.'

Aiden didn't say anything when he saw me, though I felt the brush of his gaze on my skin. I kept upright and still, imagining myself made of marble. Right through to the heart.

The interview was set up in the entertainment suite. A local independent TV production company had been hired for the original project and kept on for the new one. There was a broadcast lorry with satellite parked outside, with cables running into the basement where the cameraman and sound engineer strode around talking about angles and feeds. It was just another job for them. Lindy and I sat face to face on the stage (the statue of Artemis having been moved into the wings) with the rest of the household forming a studio audience. Even when the countdown to transmission began, I felt entirely detached from it all.

Lindy launched into her introduction. '. . . An ancient cult, dragged into the cut and thrust of modern politics. Two rival priestesses, each claiming to foretell the future. A nation in crisis, a people in need . . .'

Her voice was cosy and confiding, going over the lines we'd rehearsed so well.

'When did you first . . . ?'

'How did it feel . . . ?'

'What do you think . . . ?'

I related the story of my upbringing in the cult, my experience of the oracle and the initiation. I couldn't dazzle or charm like Cally. It didn't matter. I would be calm and certain. True.

At last we approached the end of the interview. Lindy arranged her face in suitably serious expression. 'You've made some very serious accusations. Fraud, abuse, treason.'

'They are serious, yes. I stand by them all.'

'But you're not the first to make such allegations public.'

This hadn't been in the script. 'What do you mean?' I asked.

'There was an incident during the Festival of the Goddess. I'm sure you remember it.'

She turned in her chair to face the screen behind us.

Static fizzed then settled into a clip from the news coverage of our procession. The shouting man with the staring dark eyes and wild brown curls filled the screen.

'*For shame!*' he cried. '*Liars and frauds!*'

The jostling crowd, the flickering torchlight. Opis, upright and dignified. Me and Cally, side by side among the huddled handmaidens. Seb, glaring from under King Brutus's gold wreath.

'*The Holy One sees your crimes! You have silenced her voice! Stolen the oracle!*'

The snakes spilled on to the ground, writhed and hissed.

Cries . . . shrieks . . . Opis's eyes, so steady and cold . . .

Finally the screen returned to blank.

'You witnessed this disturbance?' Lindy asked.

'Yes. At the time, everyone thought he was a lunatic.'

'And now?'

I shrugged. I felt uneasy. I was newly conscious of the invisible audience watching on their TV and computer screens. At least the studio lights meant I couldn't see Aiden and Scarlet and the rest properly. 'I don't know who that man was, or his connection to the cult. But, in light of recent events, I'd say his accusations were justified.'

Lindy nodded. 'I've been informed that the man's name is Harry Soames and that he was once a senior Trinovantum Councillor.'

There was a long pause, although she kept smiling. Sweat prickled on the back of my neck. Something was wrong. I didn't want to hear her next words. Behind the cosiness, her eyes were greedy, sharp.

'I have also been told that he is your father.'

Marble, I told myself. You are made of marble. A vessel for the goddess, that is all. You can't feel any of this.

'How did you come by that information?' By some miracle, my voice was steady.

'The same source who told me that your mother was a priestess of the Cult of Artemis, who received an oracle before her untimely death.'

Lindy put a plump hand on my knee, with an expression of simpering concern. 'I understand this must be a shock.'

I tried to reply. I was going to say something cutting yet dignified. Or maybe I was going to walk out. But the screen was a blizzard of static, and Lindy's face was crackling and blurring too. My breaths came fast and shallow.

'Aura? Aura, honey? Are you unwell?'

Her words came from very far away. The room and all the people in it were dissolving into pixels and points of light.

My head seethed, as if a nest of vipers was squirming in my skull. And through the hissing I heard a whisper: sensual, lingering.

The whisper brushed against my ear, along my skin and round my throat. Now it was a hiss, and the hiss had scales.

There was a snake coiled round my neck. It squeezed my throat, lovingly at first, then hard enough to crush the breath out of my body, the life out of my soul.

And, though I had no breath left to do it, I began to laugh.

The pressure round my throat lifted. I put out my arms and saw that they were covered in green-black scales. I'd shed my skin to reveal the serpent beneath. I laughed again, flickering my forked tongue, and slid on my belly along the dank earth of the underworld.

I was the Python.

I was the Pythia.

I spoke for the dead –

*   *   *

I woke up in the bar, laid out on a leather couch. Aiden was next to me, tapping away on a laptop.

'You know,' he said as I blinked at him woozily, 'we really should stop meeting like this.'

'How long have I been out?'

'Over an hour. It's not surprising – that was quite a performance.'

'What . . . what did I say?'

'You made this weird choking-laughing sound and said in the Game of Triumphs the Second Trump will send the Twelfth Trump swinging.'

I looked at him, confused. 'Second and twelfth what?'

'Apparently the Game of Triumphs is an old name for tarot cards. The second trump card in the deck is called the High Priestess, and the twelfth is called the Hanged Man. So it sounds like your card-playing goddess has predicted a death by hanging. Tomorrow.'

I rubbed my aching head. To the viewers at home, I was sure the oracle would have looked like a ratings-chasing stunt. After all, it wasn't as if the prophecy was something people could act on. It was just another of the goddess's games.

The worst of it was that I found it hard to care. Murder and mayhem was everywhere, yet right now all I could think about was my father. Alleged father. Alleged mother. Alleged oracle.

'Does Lindy really know who my dad was? Or was she just stirring?'

Aiden grimaced. 'Gutter journalism.'

'Yes, but is it true?'

He grimaced again. 'I don't know. Maybe. When I challenged her afterwards, she said it was Noah who gave her the tip-off. I – I'm really sorry, Aura. That was one hell of an ambush.'

'It's fine,' I said brusquely, digging my nails into my palms. The pain was steadying. 'I already knew my mother was dead. As for the rest . . . well . . . it's not like I ever expected my family to be one of the happily-ever-after kind.'

It used to be that a priestess who was caught with a man was buried alive. The rules weren't so clear for modern times. I visualised some awful prison-style reformatory in the back of beyond. Then I remembered Lindy's reference to 'untimely death', and felt another twist in my gut.

I got up and went to get a glass of water. In the mirror behind the bar, I could see that Chrystal's handiwork was pretty much intact. My skin still had a moon-shiny sheen, my eyeliner was smudge-free. I realised I could hear music. *Thump, thud, thump.*

'Sounds like a party.'

'Rick says it's for the goddess. You should make an appearance before things get too out of hand.'

'What do you mean?'

'I mean that this is a great opportunity for you to get your message across in person. Show your face, speak to people, circulate. I can help with the introductions. And speak to Noah –'

'I'll come out later. I need to lie down in my room for a bit first.'

Aiden started to say something else, but I was out of the door and into the lift before he finished. I had no intention of going to my room; I just wanted to cross-examine Noah without Aiden to distract me. I was finding it increasingly difficult to think clearly when he was around. Besides, this was something I needed to do for myself.

I walked through the angled glass-and-mirrored hall. Outside, three girls of about my age were riotously splashing about in the swimming pool. There was a DJ presiding over a sound system, and trestles of booze. The garden beyond was lit by flickering braziers and thronged with more laughing strangers. A line of people was dancing a conga across the lawn.

Rick Moodie broke free from the conga and stumbled towards me. His eyes were manic and bright. He was wearing a red leather waistcoat and ripped jeans splattered with black paint. 'Honoured Ladyship! I prophesised your prophecy! I'm an oracle too!' He gave a whoop. 'Wham, bam, thank you, *ma'am!*'

I stared at him. 'Did you actually hear what I said? About the Hanged Man, and the burial?'

'Ah, but that's the nature of artistic inspiration, ducky. Blood, sweat, tears. They say it's always darkest before dawn.' He did a little caper and grinned, waving his wrinkly little hands. 'You're me guest of honour tonight. You and Holy Artemis, here at me festival. Come and meet your followers. Give them your blessing, ducky. Have a dance. Even better – have a drink.'

He thrust a foaming glass of champagne in my hand and slung his arm round my shoulder. 'We got something to celebrate, ain't we? This here's only the beginning. You and me, we'll show 'em how it's done. We'll build a temple to be proud of, we'll found a cult worth joining –'

Two girls drew him back into the conga line. He pranced away, spraying champagne into their shrieking mouths.

Scarlet was standing a short distance away. I thought she was going to pretend she hadn't seen me, but I said her name before she could move off.

'Oh, hi,' she said stiffly. 'Congratulations on the show. It was very . . . er . . . um . . .'

'Who *are* all these people?' I asked. 'Where have they come from?'

'A busload of groupies turned up half an hour ago. As for the rest – the TV crew and their mates, a bunch of locals. The catering team Chrystal called in.'

So much for keeping my location a secret. I downed the glass of champagne without tasting it.

'I'm looking for Noah. Have you seen him?'

Scarlet seemed relieved I was moving on. She pointed to a clump of pampas grass. Noah was behind it, talking to Lindy Ryan. 'Here's the star of the show,' he said as I marched over, and flashed his toothy grin.

'Freak show, you mean,' I said. 'You set me up. Both of you.'

Lindy gave a forced laugh. 'I was just doing my job, honey. You stick to yours.' Her voice was uncertain, though, and she avoided my eye. She was frightened, I realised, as she backed away into the throng. Scarlet had been nervous of me too. It gave me a sour satisfaction.

'Quite some wrap party, huh?' said Noah, chomping at his cigar obliviously.

'Our host says it's a religious festival.'

'Well, I'm sure he'll have a few more converts after your TV debut. Swear to God, you gave me goose pimples. How d'you make your voice go like that?'

'Like what?'

'The disembodied effect. Very spooky, very cool. And that crazy laughter! Ventriloquism, am I right? Seriously, we should talk. You and Lindy have made all the major news channels. And you could go further, hit the big time. What you need –'

'I need to talk about my father. Alleged father, that is.'

'Ah.' He sleeked back his hair. 'OK. Sure.'

I waited. 'Well?'

'Well, after Mr Soames and his snakes stole the show at your festival, a pal of mine who's in PR was interested in representing him. Professionally, you know. He was all set to go to the press on Mr Soames's behalf – give his side of the story and so on. And it was a good story by all accounts. I mean, a sex scandal in the cult is bound to shift a lot of newsprint.'

'So Mr Soames told your PR friend that he'd had a child with a priestess of Artemis?'

'Right. He also claimed that his girlfriend had been in cahoots with the goddess. You know – a hotline to Mount Olympus, just like you.' He winked broadly. 'But before he could be persuaded to dish the dirt Mr Soames skipped bail and then came the coup. That's when my pal decided it was time to start over somewhere else. Last I heard he was holed up with his second wife in the South of France.'

'And what happened to my – to Mr Soames?'

'No idea.'

I longed to take him by the shoulders and shake him until all his teeth fell out. 'What about my mother? Do you know how she died?'

'Sorry, sweetheart. Haven't a clue.'

I bet Leto did, I thought. She'd known both my parents. My father, the man who meant trouble. My mother, who'd had a rebel spark. And an oracle too, allegedly . . . How much did Leto know, and how much had she concealed from me? I turned away from Noah, shoulders slumped.

It was easy to disappear, for the garden was even more confusing than the house. There were clipped hedges planted in zigzag lines, lawns set at strange angles and a maze of tiered paths. Brightly coloured lanterns hung from the trees; the woodland beyond was dark and rustling.

My head throbbed, while the smell of smoke and roasting meat from the barbecue turned my stomach. I kept rubbing my arms surreptitiously, to check for scales. Although the oracle was over, my feeling of foreboding was stronger than ever. I kept returning to the old proverbs: *Those whom the gods love die young.* And, *Those whom the gods wish to destroy, they first send mad.*

My mother had given a prophecy, and had a child. She was a priestess who broke her vows. Perhaps the goddess had chosen to destroy her.

Aiden had once described the oracle as a demonic possession. How much longer could I stay close to him, yet keep my demons at bay?

CHAPTER 16

The Emergency Committee has dismissed recent demonstrations in London, Glasgow and Cardiff as the work of a few fringe radicals. It urges the public to support its efforts to restore order to Britain's streets.

A number of the protests were in support of the ousted prime minister, Nicholas Riley. To avoid further disturbances, Riley is to be transferred from HM Prison Belmarsh to a secret location outside of London tonight.

BBC News

Back at the house, Crystal came out on to the terrace with a basket of animal masks with gilded snouts and sequined whiskers and began passing them out. Rick was wearing an antler headdress, which at least made him easy to spot, and so avoid. I was finding it increasingly hard to avoid attention myself. People had started to point and stare, though for the moment they were keeping a slightly nervous distance, as if I was an exotic animal that might bite.

I decided a mask would help. I saw one lying discarded on a flower bed, a grey wolfish creature made of papier mâché. I still felt uncomfortably exposed, however, and finally took refuge in a greenhouse.

I wasn't left in peace for long.

'The man throws his parties like he writes his music – no cliché unturned.' Aiden was standing at the door, a gold leopard mask pushed back over his tawny hair. 'Have you noticed that whenever people say they admire the pagans it's just an excuse to get wasted in fancy dress?'

He looked more relaxed than I'd seen for a while. I realised I'd missed his mocking smile. Although it made my stomach flutter, I tried to keep my tone light-hearted too. 'Rick has got his gods confused. Artemis isn't exactly famous for her partying. It's Dionysus who was the crazy hedonist.'

'Maybe you should consider a change of cult. Why are you hiding anyway? This is all in your honour.'

I went to join him at the doorway of the greenhouse and surveyed the scene. It was a long way from the drinks receptions at the High Priestess's residence. Everyone looked as if they were on some kind of high, many were in various states of undress and the music was loud enough to make your ears bleed. 'They're Rick Moodie's groupies, not mine.'

'Only some of them. Most of the people here watched your TV interview and then came to find you. Word's got out – there are more arriving all the time.'

'Great. I bet the Civil Guard won't be far behind.'

'So maybe it's time to stop hiding. This could be your chance. Yes, some people are here just to have a good time. But others want inspiration. Leadership. They want to believe in you.'

I swallowed hard. 'Do you believe in me?'

'In every way.' Aiden's smile wasn't mocking any more. 'Even if you weren't the oracle, I'd want you to be a part of this. I'd still want you with me. Do you understand?'

I didn't know how to answer. Maybe I didn't need to. I just looked back at him, shivers running up and down my spine.

'You're a girl worth believing in, Aura. You're worth fighting for.'

We had been talking loudly, to hear ourselves over the music. Abruptly, it cut out. With a clash of cymbals, and a raucous shout, Rick called the revellers to follow him. There was a white-painted gazebo on top of a small hill in the centre of the garden. He sprang up the steps and under the arches, banging the cymbals and skipped about as his guests milled below. Crystal and Seraphina, both very unsteady on their feet, waved flaming torches to either side. They looked like a couple of cut-price priestesses in flowing white dresses, flowers stuck in their hair. Scarlet watched, arms folded and expression inscrutable, from the side.

'Welcome, my friends,' Rick bellowed, raising his hands to the heavens. 'Welcome to the Holy Feast of the Goddess of the Moon!'

He plunged into slurred ramblings about his muse, the moon and why the goddess had marked us all for greatness. His audience shuffled restlessly.

I still felt light-headed, but it was more than the disorientating effects of the oracle. I'd left the tangle of fears about death and madness behind, and was buzzing with different emotions. Emotions that I found it hard to separate from the champagne and the lights swinging in the trees . . . And Aiden, smiling and sardonic at my side.

Aiden, who believed in me. Who didn't just think I was a Cause or a Project or whatever else Scarlet had said.

He was right: these people were here for me and Artemis, not some has-been rock star. It was time for me to take charge. It was time for me to prove that, yes, I *was* someone worth fighting for.

I ran up the slope and grabbed the microphone off Rick. He did a bleary double take. 'Honoured Worshipfulness!'

I wore the wolf-mask on my head, like a crown. My silk dress swished around my ankles, the body shimmer sparkled on my face and throat and arms. A lot of the guests were preoccupied with their drinks and each other. But the ones gathering at the front were gazing up at me with a hopeful, hungry sort of look. They were quiet and ready to listen. Many were holding up camera phones.

My voice rang out, loud and confident.

'I am Aura. I am the Oracle of Artemis. I am *your* oracle – the one the cult and the Emergency Committee want to hide from you. Don't listen to their lies. Don't believe their promises. Artemis sees them for what they are: tyrants and traitors.'

It was hard to speak over the whoops and cheers. But my voice rose above it all. This time, it wasn't the goddess speaking. This was me.

'If you want to protect the true oracle, if you care about the freedom of our country, don't let them get away with this. Strike, protest, disrupt. Malcolm Greeve is going to the temple for a private oracle this week – let's show him what we think of him, and his friends' fake prophecies. It's time to reclaim our temple, and our streets.'

I had everyone's attention now. Their roars of support were deafening.

'The world is watching, and so is the goddess. I'll be with you. Artemis will be with you. Together –'

There was another clash of the cymbals. Rick had pushed in front of me, grinning manically. '*Viva la revolución!*'

'Revolution! Revolution!' the crowd bellowed back.

'All hail the Queen of Beasts!' he cried. 'Let us revel in her darkness! Let us dance in her light!' He flung back his head and began to howl. 'Let the wild hunt begin!' The music was back with a thrash of metal and drums.

People began to leap and run around the garden, barking like dogs and pretending to blow horns. Aiden was at my side, but I hardly heard what he said. I backed into the gazebo, suddenly frightened by the horde of people crowding the hill.

Many still wore masks; those with bare faces had a frenzied gleam in their eyes. I glimpsed Lindy Ryan, her dress half pulled off her shoulders, hair wild, stumbling about and laughing hysterically. I felt a tremble of hysteria too.

'Come on,' said Aiden in my ear. 'Let's get away from all this.'

He ushered me away from the crowd and towards the gate in the wrought-iron fence that separated the garden from the wood. I hung back, but not for long. This time the darkness of the wood was inviting, the air cool and full of whisperings.

The lights from the house glowed behind a web of leaves. The trees were black, the sky bronze. The party's thumping music and muffled shrieks seemed to belong to another world. My head was spinning and my skin prickled; I didn't know if it was excitement or dread. Somehow it seemed that this was where I'd been meant to be from the start of everything. That this place, this person, this moment had always been waiting for me.

Aiden and I stood facing each other. We hadn't hurried, yet both of us were out of breath.

'Everyone's gone mad,' I said. 'Maybe the spirit of Dionysus is here after all.'

'It's just us. Only us.'

He meant that the craziness of the party was all too human. But I wanted him to mean something else. That the two of us were alone together and no one was watching, not even a god.

I took a step closer. So did he. His face was shadow-dappled, his eyes greener than the leaves.

I would allow myself to touch him. Just the once. I reached up and traced the strong arch of his brows, the curve of his cheek, the hollows of his neck. His skin was warm bronze. I let my hand fall, and stepped back. Never again.

'Aura . . .'

'I can't,' I whispered. 'I mustn't. The goddess –'

'I understand, but you have to listen.' Aiden moved closer, his voice urgent yet coaxing. 'I know you have a gift – call it second sight or an extra-developed sixth sense. Hell, maybe it's even down to a rip in the space–time continuum. But the only reason you see Artemis in your visions is because that's what you expect to see. Your whole life's been built around her mythology, and so that's what your brain uses to make sense of the experience. The goddess can't actually hurt you. She can't hurt anyone. Otherwise, why are Opis and Lionel still strutting around the temple?'

'Artemis doesn't care about them. She chose *me*. I'm bound to her now, forever.' I took a deep, shaking breath.

'Do you know what happened to the first Aura, the one I'm named after? She was a handmaiden who claimed to be even more pure than Artemis. As revenge, Artemis caused her to be raped by the god Dionysus. It sent her mad. She gave birth to twin sons, and ate one of them. She –'

'Horror stories and old wives' tales. Forget them.'

I was in his arms. He felt strong. He felt safe. I clutched at him with cold fingers.

'You should be frightened too. Look at Orion. The goddess loved him, but when he seduced one of her nymphs she killed him. Don't you see? The British made Orion into Herne, but the story's the same.' I was babbling. I knew I didn't make sense any more but my fear was gushing out with the words, unstoppable. 'You're my Lord Herne. You've been Chosen too. Like Orion. The hunter turned into prey. Like Actaeon –'

'Listen to me.' Aiden gripped me by the shoulders. 'I don't care. Even if Artemis is real, even if she's picked me, I don't choose *her*. If those old tales are true, then she doesn't deserve to be worshipped.'

He tried to smile at me, but the smile was crooked. His lips would taste of blasphemy, dark and intoxicating. I could taste it in my mouth too. The taste of freedom, the taste of all forbidden things.

I leaned in and I kissed him, right on his forbidden mouth. It was as warm and hungry as mine. We fell to the ground, entangled, pulling at each other's clothes, grasping at each other's hair. Earth and leaves rolled damply against my skin.

He kept saying my name. 'Aura. Oh, Aura.'

Then I heard it again. *Aura.*

And with it, I felt a cold breath on my skin, a sick heat in my blood. A chiming in my head and all through my bones.

I flung Aiden off me with a shout: of anger or terror, I didn't know.

We stared at each other, motionless. Only a short distance away, voices from the party were raised in yelps and howls. There was a moment of perfect, scorching clarity.

And then night poured into me, black and infinite, and the moon blazed in my skull.

I was breaking into pieces, fragments of light and leaves. I would break Aiden into pieces too. I would hear him howl. I would flay his flesh. I would pluck out his eyes, I would tear at the pulp of his heart and brain –

Please. No. Have mercy.

I lurched upwards and away.

Forgive me. Forgive him. I beg –

I had some confused idea of drawing the goddess away from Aiden, into the trees. For how could they hurt me, I thought dazedly, when they were only painted leaves? Then the painted web turned into a real one, the branches whipping my face, briars tearing my clothes. I sobbed and gasped as horror snapped at my heels.

I seemed to run for hours, days, pursued by the goddess's fury. Once, I saw the dead animals of Artemisia House had escaped their glass cases and come to life in the undergrowth. I smelled their decayed breath and dusty pelts, heard them snarl as they bared their yellowed fangs. Another time, I tripped over a bramble that became a thin black serpent, coiled round my leg. It bit my leg so the blood ran, and I realised the whole forest floor was squirming with snakes. Yet I stumbled on.

When I came to my senses, the wood had thinned, and I was standing beside a tarmacked road. Above me, the moon was full; bright and hard as ice.

Those whom the gods love die young.

Those whom the gods wish to destroy, they first send mad.

The goddess loves me . . . and so she sends me mad.

The goddess hates me . . . and so she sends me mad.

She loves me, she loves me not. She loves me, she –

*　*　*

Silence. Black and silver trees, black road, silver girl. The moon, the moon.

I turned and saw Aiden in the shadows of the wood.

'It was the goddess,' I said, quite calmly. 'She was going to kill you. I was going to kill you.'

He made a slow, uncertain step towards me. At once I shouted out with a violence that cracked my voice: 'Stay back! Back –'

I fled down the road, into the night.

CHAPTER 17

Police sources have confirmed that the prime minister,
Nicholas Riley, was found hanging from a lamp post
in Trafalgar Square at five o'clock this morning.

    The prime minister was being transferred
between prisons when a group of masked gunmen
attacked the van in which he and his guards were
travelling. No group has yet claimed responsibility for
the atrocity.

BBC News

'Whatever happened to you?'

It was Scarlet, leaning out of her sports car in the light of a thin yellow dawn. I'd been wandering the road for hours, barely noticing the surrounding blur of fields and pylons, sheep and trees.

She was looking at me curiously. I remembered that my hands and face were flecked with blood, that my dress was torn, my hair wild.

'It was the goddess,' I said at last. 'She came to me again, in a vision. And then I, er, decided to go for a walk. To clear my head.'

'Well, I've been looking for you.'

'Did . . . did Aiden ask you to?'

'I haven't seen him since the party.' Scarlet drummed her fingers distractedly on the wheel. 'Look, don't take this the wrong way or anything, but I think that maybe you coming to stay with us was a mistake after all. Dad totally lost it last night. And, well, now that so many people know you're here it won't be safe. For any of us.'

She didn't meet my eye. Despite her offhand tone, I knew she was afraid. The goddess and I had given her more than she'd bargained for.

'It's OK,' I said. 'I was leaving anyway. Artemis has a new task for me, and Aiden can't be involved. The goddess wants me to do this alone.'

Her relief was obvious. 'Great. I mean, it's great that the goddess is guiding you. Because your prophecy's already been proved true. It was the prime minister – did you know? He was found an hour ago, swinging from a lamp post. It's just been on the news.'

'Oh.'

'Horrible, isn't it? The Emergency Committee says it was another terrorist attack, but it's more likely they arranged it themselves.'

'I'm sure you're right.' It didn't seem real, or particularly important.

'So, uh, what are you going to do now? Is there anything I can do to help?'

Good question. It was time to pull myself together. Time, too, to exploit Scarlet's guilt at getting rid of me. I'd start by finding Leto, I thought. I had a lot of questions for her.

'Actually, I could do with a change of clothes and something to eat. And is there any chance you could give me a lift into London?'

'Of course.' Scarlet was brimming over with helpfulness. 'I'll get you some cash too. I can even give you the keys to my mother's flat. She's in the States at the moment so you won't be disturbed.'

'That's very kind.'

She gave an over-bright smile. 'No problem at all.'

Twenty minutes later, she returned with clothes and a baseball cap, plus a small bag of essentials. Once we set off, I stretched out in the back seat of the car and closed my eyes, willing the last few days to dissolve into fantasy and forgetfulness. I had to tell myself it was all a dream. If I was to remember the warmth of Aiden's hands, the scent of his hair, his breath on my neck, then I would also have to remember my crazed run through the woods. I was awake now and returned to sanity. I mustn't defy the goddess again.

The main roads into central London were subject to checkpoints, so I asked Scarlet to drop me off in a quiet suburban street. From there, I was going to get a bus and trust my luck it wouldn't be pulled over for a stop-and-search.

'Are you sure you'll be OK?' she asked.

'Artemis will protect me.'

After the woods, I knew that for certain. Possessed by the goddess, I was armed and dangerous. Untouchable.

Scarlet cleared her throat. She still couldn't look me in the eye. 'What should I tell Aiden?'

'Keep him with you. Don't let him come to London – it's not safe.' I had no way of explaining that the danger wasn't London, but me. Me and the goddess. 'And tell him . . . tell him I'm sorry.'

This was as much as I could manage. I got out of the car without saying thank you or even goodbye. I couldn't bear for her to hear the break in my voice.

Not so long ago, the idea of navigating the city on my own would have terrified me. Now I was simply grateful to be alone and anonymous on its streets. I had money and a place to stay, thanks to Scarlet's guilt trip. I even had a plan, of sorts. Just one step forward. And another.

Don't think too much about it, I told myself, tugging the baseball cap down over my forehead. *Don't think about anything. Just keep going.*

I boarded the right bus, without attracting so much as a second glance from my fellow passengers. I even managed to get off at the right stop. I gazed up at the British Museum's parade of columns and pediment and felt briefly comforted. It was designed just like a Greek temple.

Since the riots, most of the museum's major exhibits had been moved to a secret location for safe keeping. Still, the fact that so many of its staff had been laid off would be to my advantage. I trusted in Artemis to keep me hidden and was waved through security with the rest of the queue. We poured into the museum's Great Court, under the milky light of its billowing steel-and-glass roof.

The cult had been instrumental in founding the museum, and so priestesses have always had a token role in curating the ancient Greek artefacts. As I made my way to the Greek pottery room, I could only hope that the usual roster for this was still in operation.

My luck was in: there was no attendant on guard. And after only fifteen minutes of examining a case of Athenian vases I saw a veiled woman emerge from the back office. I knew from the eyes, large and watery green, that I'd got the right priestess.

'Cynthia. It's me.'

She started violently.

'*Aura?* No. No, I can't talk to you. It's forbidden.'

She backed away, eyes darting wildly. I'd taken a big risk. But when I was little Cynthia had been especially kind to me. Playing games, telling stories, saving me sweets. Until the night she was initiated as a priestess, and everything changed.

I pressed on. 'Have you heard about the films I've been making? The accusations I've made against the cult?'

She gave the tiniest of nods. I'd been fairly certain that even the most ruthless crackdown couldn't keep the Sanctuary gossip-free, but the news still came as a relief.

'Do you believe I was speaking the truth? The truth about my initiation night?'

Another tiny nod. Her hands twitched. I could tell she wanted to suck her thumb.

I let out a long wavering sigh. 'Can we talk somewhere, then? Please?'

After an anxious survey of the room, Cynthia led me into one of the museum's service corridors. It was ill-lit and, for now, deserted.

'After you ran away,' she said, whispering so quietly I strained to hear her, 'we all got interviewed by the police. Everyone's saying you're a criminal. That you've been cursed by the goddess.'

'I think you know who the real criminals are. The cult, the council, the coup – they're all connected. They've hurt a lot of people and they have to be stopped.'

She flushed. 'Phoebe's left the cult, you know. Her family came and collected her. I heard them shouting at Opis.'

I wondered about the other girls I'd left behind in the Sanctuary: Iphigenia and Arethusa, the twins. They didn't have anyone to take them away.

'I'm really sorry to involve you,' I said. 'I know there are all sorts of people looking for me and I don't want you to get into trouble. But I really need to get a message to Leto and I'm kind of out of options.'

Cynthia gazed at me with wide green eyes, eyes that had once danced with liveliness. 'I tried to run away too, you know.'

'It was different for me,' I said gently. 'Easier. I had help.'

'The goddess would want me to help you, wouldn't she?'

I nodded, suppressing a stab of guilt. My reasons for contacting Leto were selfish. Only Leto could tell me the truth about my mother and father.

Exposing Opis and overthrowing the Emergency Committee was still my priority. But now I had another burning need: to free myself of Artemis. That was why I had to find out about my mother's oracle. I had to know if she'd escaped the goddess before she died.

CHAPTER 18

The Emergency Committee has issued a statement strongly condemning the lynching of the prime minister, Nicholas Riley, and assuring the nation that those responsible will be brought to justice. General Ferrer rejected claims that the committee was involved in the hanging as 'sheer fantasy'.

The leader of the committee, Malcolm Greeve, has confirmed he will visit the Temple of Artemis tomorrow for a private oracle. However, he was unable to set a date for the re-call of Parliament, citing on-going security concerns.

BBC News

Scarlet's mother, a part-time actress who lived in LA, obviously hadn't used her London flat for a long time. The air smelled stale and there were dust sheets over the furniture. Most of the other apartments in the luxury development were unoccupied. The building's silence was eerie. Before going to bed, I switched on the TV, partly to have some background noise, and saw a repeat of Cally announcing her last oracle, the one promising sunshine and rainbows and treats for all. She was sitting on a gold throne next to Opis, dolled-up like some kind of film star. I wondered if she was enjoying herself.

The shock of the last twenty-four hours had worn off; I couldn't numb my thoughts any more. I lay on the bed, staring into the dark, and felt more alone than I ever had in my life.

Whenever I closed my eyes, I saw Aiden's face as he looked at me for the last time. Did he think me a freak? A madwoman? Possessed by demons? I didn't blame him. I hardly knew myself.

I kept thinking of another famous oracle: the Sibyl of Cumae. She asked the gods to live a thousand years, but forgot to ask for youth to go with it. So she got older and older, until she was so tiny and wizened she was kept in a jar. In the end, only her voice was left, with which she begged to die. Aiden would dismiss this as just another fairy tale. But I could imagine what a lifetime spent listening to the goddess would do to the body and soul. A lifetime shut away from the ordinary world. A lifetime unloved, untouched, by mortal hands.

It was better in the morning, as it always is. I went to check the drop-off I'd agreed with Cynthia: a bench outside the British Museum. There was an envelope taped to the underside of its slats with a note from Leto. Somewhat to my surprise, she had agreed to see me. We were to meet that afternoon, in plenty of time before the curfew, at an address in West London.

I wasn't the only person to be hunched over and covered up, eyes fixed on the ground. Nobody wanted to draw attention to themselves. CCTV cameras were everywhere and there seemed to be more than a usual number of police officers on the streets. Along the way, I saw a bow and arrow spraypainted on a wall. The arrow pointed to my name, Aura, written in large wobbly red letters. I knew I should be encouraged by this show of popular support. Instead, I felt like I was walking around with a giant bulls-eye tattooed on my forehead.

However, my goddess-given luck continued to hold and I didn't run into any checkpoints, arriving at the address only ten minutes late. The neighbourhood was wealthy enough to have escaped the rash of boarded-up windows and smashed-up cars. I made my way to an upmarket mansion block and looked at the name listed for Flat 6: Miss P. Smith.

Leto's querulous voice answered the intercom. She didn't buzz me in but came down to the lobby. She was dressed in her usual black tracksuit, her usual scowl on her face.

'I'm not at your beck and call just because you're on first-name terms with our Higher Power,' she said before I could even open my mouth. 'The only reason I agreed to meet was because I wanted to put a stop to your pestering.'

I couldn't stop grinning. I hadn't realised I would be so happy to see her. 'How are you? I was worried that you'd got into trouble. I was worried that Opis and the rest would suspect you after I escaped.'

She snorted. 'One of the few advantages of being old – everyone reckons you're daft to boot.'

'So you didn't have problems getting away this afternoon?'

'Why should I? This is a regular appointment.'

I remembered that Leto did, in fact, use to disappear every Thursday afternoon. I'd plucked up the courage to ask her about it once and she'd muttered something about visiting the sick. I hadn't been sure if it was a joke. The cult's charitable efforts were mostly restricted to food parcels and fundraising galas.

I followed her up the stairs to Number 6 and the mysterious Miss Smith. We found the flat's occupant lying on a daybed under the window. Trying to cover my surprise, I touched my fingers to my brow.

'Honoured Apollonia.'

The ex-High Priestess shook her head. 'Call me Polly, my dear. We don't stand on ceremony here.'

The last time I'd seen her was at Opis's dinner party. At the time, I'd thought she seemed unwell, and she looked worse now. Though in her mid sixties, she still possessed a dainty prettiness. But her skin was waxy and her hands shook. The table by the daybed was littered with bottles of pills.

I didn't want to feel pity. Apollonia/Polly would have known both my mother and father. She'd been a regular if infrequent visitor to the Sanctuary as I was growing up and yet, like Leto, she had never thought to tell me where I had come from.

The flat showed no sign of the goddess or its owner's former vocation. It was large and plush and covered in chintz. China figurines of cats, clowns and girls in ballgowns crammed every available surface. Leto set about giving the ornaments a disapproving dust.

Our former leader smiled at her weakly. 'You're so good to me.'

'Hmph. It's the extra channels on the telly I come for,' said Leto. 'And the interweb thingy. Poll's downstairs neighbour is one of those technical types,' she told me. 'Used to work in IT. He set us up with all the right equipment, showed us how the buttons work.'

So this was how Leto got round the Sanctuary's news censorship.

'That was quite a speech you gave, missy,' she continued. 'Standing up on that hill, yelling at everyone to protest against the fake oracle and tell the committee where to shove it . . . Which is all well and good, except that it won't be you shut up in the temple with a baying mob outside.'

I sat down on a floral-sprigged armchair and looked at them both. 'If you saw my speech, then you must have seen my interview with Lindy Ryan.'

'Yes, and it was *most* upsetting.' Polly squeezed her eyes shut. 'Oh, gracious. I wish we didn't have to drag all this business up. Really, after all these years, what good can it possibly do?'

'The truth has a way of coming out,' Leto said grimly. 'I said it then, and I say it now.'

I nodded encouragingly, even though I was burning with impatience. Here I was, finally about to learn the secret of my birth. The secret of my mother's death. And maybe, just maybe, the secret of how to get rid of Artemis . . .

'I tried my best,' Polly mumbled. 'I really did. But it was always drama, with those two girls.'

'Which two? Opis and – and my mother?'

'That's right, dear. Opis and Carya.'

My mother's name. A priestess's name. Unmistakable yet anonymous.

'Like chalk and cheese, they were. Came from such different backgrounds, you see. I always said it was a mistake, letting in charity cases. The cult has always been for the elite.'

Leto rolled her eyes as Polly rambled on. 'Opis, of course, came from a very good family. One of our finest. Your mother, on the other hand, came to us from foster care at the age of nine, on the recommendation of her social worker. It seemed a good idea at the time. She was such a bright little thing. Do you remember, Leto?'

'I do,' she said shortly. 'There was quite a mouth on her. Always coming up with some scheme or a fanciful notion. Whereas Opis stood on her dignity even as a girl. She took everything very seriously in those days.'

It was difficult to imagine Opis as a child. And strange, too, to find that my mother's personality – mouthy, assertive – was so different to mine.

Polly plucked at her blanket. 'The funny thing is, they were both popular, in their different ways. When I came to retire, and we held elections for my successor, I was surprised to find the votes were split. Of course the final decision was mine. I prayed to the goddess for guidance, but she was silent.' She sighed. 'Always silent . . . Anyway. It seemed clear that Opis would be the better ambassador for the cult. I was confident I made the right decision.'

Her eyes fluttered closed. I worried she was slipping into a dose. A delay would be unbearable. I leaned towards her. 'So what happened next?'

'Carya,' said Leto, 'claimed to have an oracle.'

It was what I expected, yet my heart still seemed to skip a beat. 'What about?'

'Oh, some nonsense about the temple being a nest of snakes,' said Polly fretfully.

I closed my eyes, saw the Festival Day crowd in Temple Square, the knot of serpents wriggling on the ground.

Polly, however, was oblivious. 'I'm sure, even now, that it was just to cause mischief. A bid for attention. There was only one witness: a young Trinovantum Councillor named Harry Soames. He was a family friend of Opis's, in fact.'

Of course, I thought. *That was why he knew her Christian name.*

'Three days before I was due to step down formally, Harry came to me and said he was going to call a meeting of the Trinovantum Council, to propose that Carya should replace Opis. He wanted to make the oracle public too.'

'What did the council say?'

'The meeting was never held. That same day, I discovered that Carya was pregnant. She'd managed to hide it for nearly six months, goodness knows how. But then she had some kind of fainting episode. It was Leto who found her, lying at the bottom of the stairs. I nearly collapsed myself – from the shock, you know. Dreadful, it was. Yet in some ways, it made everything simple. A fallen woman – a disgraced priestess – couldn't possibly have been favoured with an oracle. It was confirmation she'd made it up.

'Really, it was all so *sordid*.' Polly reached out to stroke the skirts of a china shepherdess. 'You can't imagine. It was a horrible, *horrible* time. Mr Soames had the affront to tell me he'd marry the girl and the two of them would start a new life. Carya, however, wanted none of it. She was quite unhinged. She said her child was a child of the goddess alone and that both of them should continue to live in the cult. It was all we could do to persuade her to spend the rest of her pregnancy in a private clinic, away from prying eyes.'

'How . . . how did she die?' The words stuck in my throat.

Leto looked down at her hands. 'An infection set in after the birth.'

'We respected your mother's wishes,' Polly said feebly. 'She wanted you brought up in the cult. So we told your father, and the rest, that her baby had died too. We said it was a boy. Opis put you in the care of a foster family for half a year before taking you back. That way, you came to us untainted by the circumstances of your conception.'

'*Untainted*?' It took all my strength to refrain from smashing one of the shiny pastel figurines on to the floor. 'That's a joke. I was robbed of a father, of the chance of a normal life, just so the cult could keep its precious reputation.'

'We had to . . . we had to . . . protect the honour of the goddess.'

'Who knew about this?'

Leto replied, her tone as brusque as ever. 'A handful of people within the cult and council were aware of the circumstances of Carya's death. However, the only ones who knew her child had survived were myself, Polly and Opis. After learning Carya was dead, Harry Soames had a breakdown. He disappeared. None of us saw or heard anything of him until his grand comeback at the festival.'

Polly blinked up at me. 'You mustn't be angry, dear. Your mother's death was not in vain.'

'What's that supposed to mean?'

'Nothing,' said Leto sharply. 'It's all nonsense.'

Polly beckoned me to come close. 'People used to think that to renew the oracle – to strengthen the bond between human and divine – a blood sacrifice had to be made. That's why we used to make offerings of wild animals in the temple. Back in the ancient times, though, it would have been a priestess.'

I sucked in my breath. 'You mean the cult used to practise *human* sacrifice?'

'Hogwash,' said Leto.

Polly ignored her. She put her frail hands on mine. 'Blood, especially the blood of a priestess, is a powerful thing. Sacrifice calls the goddess to us. It releases her too.'

Then she sat back and gave a tremulous smile. 'Don't be afraid, Aura. Artemis Theron chose you as a sign of her mercy. The sins of the mother, absolved by the daughter. That's why she favours you with her oracles. *Real* oracles – not the rubbish that silly girl Callisto is spouting. You should be very proud.'

I shook my head. I didn't trust myself to speak. I could hardly confess that I didn't want to give oracles any more; it was supposed to be my sacred duty.

Sacrifice calls the goddess to us. It releases her too.

A shiver ran down my spine. Was that my only chance of escape? Death?

The ex-High Priestess gave a long and wavering sigh. 'I thought, once, that I had been Chosen too. So I waited and waited. Listening, always listening for a word . . . a sign . . . My whole life.' She frowned. 'But I did my best. I did my best by those girls. All my girls . . .'

Her voice was fading; her eyes closed. Leto shooed me into the hall.

'Pay no attention to that sacrifice twaddle. Poll's very ill and her mind wanders. She's always been weak . . . in both senses of the word.' The old priestess gave me an awkward pat. 'Now then. You're probably right to be angry, but it's true that Carya wanted you to be raised in the cult.

Of course, she didn't know what a tyrant Opis would turn out to be. None of us did.'

'I didn't mind being an orphan,' I said bitterly. 'Somehow this is worse.'

Leto harrumphed. Clearly, her limited sympathy was already wearing thin. 'Parents can be a mixed blessing, believe me. I joined the cult to escape mine. You're your own person. No point dwelling on the might-have-beens.'

'I can't help it.'

She harrumphed again. 'Have it your own way. He wants to meet you, for what it's worth.'

'Who?'

'Harry Soames, of course.'

I stared at her. 'You know where he is?'

'He got in touch with me after you went AWOL. He's been living abroad until recently. But somebody who'd worked at the private hospital when your mother was there finally decided to talk apparently. Now, because Mr Grease-Weasel is visiting the temple tomorrow –'

I blinked at the apparent change in subject. 'What weasel?'

'Chancellor Whatsit. The one who's supposedly heading the Emergency Committee.'

'Malcolm Greeve.'

'Like I said. Anyway, he's fixed up a private oracle from Callisto and, thanks to you, a lot of folk will be coming to the temple to protest against it. Harry's going to be among them. He wants to meet you beforehand.' Leto handed me a scrap of paper with directions. 'Seems to me I'm turning into your PA. Carrying messages, arranging your schedule . . .' She eyed me balefully. 'It'll be picking up your dry-cleaning next.'

I tried to stammer out my thanks.

'Just don't get too carried away,' she warned, prodding me towards the door. 'We don't want things to get messy.'

I didn't know whether she meant the meeting or the protest.

CHAPTER 19

Criminal gangs have been blamed for sabotaging the internet and telephone networks, resulting in extensive communication blackouts.

As a result, the Emergency Committee urges people not to attempt to attend demonstrations or any other large gatherings. For their own safety and security, citizens are advised to stay at home.

BBC News

It was time for me to make good on my promises.

I'd stood on top of a hill, decked out in silk and sparkles, and promised the people gathered to see me that I was on their side. No doubt the phone footage of my call to arms had already spread far and wide. By now, thousands of people would have heard me pledge that I would be with them, all the way. *The world is watching, and so is the goddess*, I'd said.

It was more true than they knew. Artemis was watching me, always, for signs of weakness or betrayal. Tomorrow I would confront my father. But whatever he told me, whatever fresh revelations he had, I wouldn't waver from my duty. Tomorrow I would march on the temple. Tomorrow would be a true Festival of the Goddess.

I remembered a conversation I'd had with Aiden at Rick Moodie's house. 'If General Ferrer got his way from the start,' Aiden had said, 'I reckon he would have arrested all the MPs. They'd have closed the airports and shut down all satellite communications. Stopped foreign journalists from entering the country, rounded up the independent media. This here is a coup lite. It's terribly British, really. So damn *polite*.'

Our new rulers evidently hoped that their subjects would be as polite about things as they were. But it was starting to look as if people weren't going to sit back and hope for the best. There had been daily protests outside Parliament, and now the temple was a target too. Thanks to my oracles, and my speech at Rick Moodie's party, I was partly responsible for the backlash.

And if the backlash ended in blood, I thought with a clutch of dread, I would be responsible for that too.

I was due to meet Harry – I couldn't yet think of him as my father – in a café not far from Temple Tube station. Dressed in baggy clothes, my hair scraped back, cap pulled low, I could have passed for a twelve-year-old boy. I was a long way from the girl in the television interview, with her smoky eyes and glittering cheekbones, her seductive silk dress.

I came face to face with that girl only a few blocks away on a 'wanted' poster. I didn't think it looked much like me. Further along, I saw several more graffiti tags with the bow and arrow and my name. A workman was already painting over them. Still, I supposed the omen was a good one.

Central London was closed to traffic, and public transport had been suspended due to so-called strike action, so I was in for a long walk. It was eerily quiet without the rumble of traffic or wail of sirens. My route took me through Hyde Park. The rubbish bins hadn't been emptied for weeks, the grass wasn't mown and the flower beds were overgrown with weeds. The wilderness was taking over. Yet the trees were lush and green, the sky a hopeful blue.

I'd imagined that the communication blackout, as well as the fear factor, would mean the protest was relatively small. But there was already a steady stream of people heading in the direction of the temple, many carrying home-made banners and placards. Like the streets, they were strangely quiet. No chanted slogans or songs, hardly any conversation. Their faces were silent and set.

As I pushed open the door to the café, my heart was beating so strongly I thought it would jump out of my chest. The place had only a handful of customers. I passed the tables in the main room and went, as instructed, to a small room at the back. The only person there was my father.

He was sitting at a table, nursing a mug of tea. The last time I'd seen him his eyes had been angry and staring, his hair wild. He looked thinner, greyer, than I'd remembered.

I stood in the doorway, waiting for him to look up. He lurched to his feet and the chair clattered to the floor. Without saying a word, he gripped me by the arms and looked me over intensely from top to toe.

Finally, with a sigh of disappointment, he released me. 'You don't look much like her.'

I didn't look much like him either, I thought. But his abrupt manner suited me. I wasn't ready for hugs of welcome. I picked up the fallen chair and sat down at the table. He sat down too. After a short pause, we tried to smile at each other.

'The thing is,' I said, 'I don't even know what my – what Carya looked like.'

Only the High Priestess gets her portrait painted, and since members of the cult are veiled in public and banned from taking pictures in the Sanctuary, they are never photographed barefaced. Harry Soames took out his wallet and very carefully passed me an old snapshot. It was taken at a party in the Trinovantum Council; I'd been for drinks there myself, in their wood-panelled clubroom. I thought I could see the council treasurer in the background, and the back of what might be Opis's head. And a girl with light brown hair and a laughing mouth.

She was skinny and small, like me. We had the same wide brow, perhaps. Otherwise, she was a stranger. Just like the man before me now.

'Lovely, isn't she?' he said, and there was an ache in his voice.

She looked ordinary, I thought. I didn't want to give

the photo back, but it wasn't mine, and neither was she. Not really.

'How did you get to know her?' I asked as he tucked the photo carefully away.

'We worked on some charitable projects together. It was something she thought the cult should do more of. She was proud of the cult, but there were things she wanted to change.'

'I can imagine.'

'That's why I got involved in the resistance. Carya would hate what's happened to the country. If she'd been High Priestess, she'd have been out protesting in the streets too.'

He shifted awkwardly in his seat. 'How . . . how's it been? Your life in the cult, I mean?'

'It's been OK. Good, actually. Until suddenly it wasn't.' I gave a short, embarrassed laugh. 'But I'm all right now.'

'If I'd known, I'd have come and taken you. Looked after you. You believe that, don't you? We'd have worked something out.'

'I understand. It's OK.'

He considered me again. 'You might not look much like her. But you have her spirit. That's why Artemis talks to you.'

'You witnessed her oracle?'

'I'll never forget it. I was in the presence of something holy and inhuman. I don't think I've ever been so frightened, or so exhilarated.'

I nodded. I understood.

'Carya said there was a serpent in the temple. A serpent with a forked tongue. That's why I threw the snakes at Opis, you see. She knew what they meant.' He grimaced. 'The woman's poison. And as slippery as they come.'

'Honoured Apollonia implied that my mother's death was the reason I got the gift of prophecy. She said the power of the oracle is renewed by a blood sacrifice.' And, I thought to myself, *released by sacrifice too*. But exactly how this worked was still a mystery.

Harry frowned. 'Carya wouldn't have sacrificed herself. She was a fighter. She'd have fought to live for your sake, if nothing else. She'd be fighting now – to save the name of the cult, the honour of the country. As you are. It will give people a huge boost to see you at the demonstration.'

I wasn't sure yet if I should make myself known. I was waiting for a sign. But I nodded all the same.

'Today's protest will be a turning point,' Harry said. 'Especially now that the Houses of Parliament have been closed – for security reasons, allegedly. Did you know that a group of MPs is going to meet in Westminster Abbey instead? They're gathering there this evening, to debate the latest Emergency Committee legislation. They – we – have to show the committee that civil resistance isn't going to go away.'

I had a painfully vivid vision of Aiden's face, flushed and intent, leaning close to mine as he extolled the importance of people power. I shook it away.

'Causing a ruckus outside the temple is turning out to be a family trait,' I said, trying to lighten the atmosphere. 'Like father, like daughter.'

Harry blinked at me. 'But I'm not your real father, Aura. You must know that. Don't you?'

All the breath was knocked out of me. 'Well, I thought . . . I mean . . . that's what Leto and Apollonia . . .'

He was shaking his head. 'No. I'm so sorry. Really – I didn't realise they'd misunderstood. It was such a confusing, terrible time . . . You see, I said I'd marry Carya and care for the child. But Carya and I were never lovers.'

'But you – but she –'

'She didn't feel like I did. When the scandal of her pregnancy broke, I still wanted to protect her. I wanted to take her and her baby away from the cult.' He took my hand. 'I loved her. I would have loved you.'

I pulled my hand away. 'If you're not my father, then who is?'

'She said the goddess gave you to her. That was all. Carya was the true oracle though. She spoke for Artemis. Maybe we should believe her.'

His curls were sticking up all over the place, his eyes bright with conviction. A nice man. But he was only really interested in me for what I'd inherited from my mother.

The child of a virgin goddess, born to a virgin priestess . . . Well, it was no more impossible than the other impossible things that had happened to me.

I stood up abruptly. I felt emptied out, hollow with this new loss. 'It was nice meeting you. And, er, thank you. For talking and everything. And helping my mother. But I'd better get to the demonstration. The chancellor will be at the temple soon.'

'You don't have to leave just yet. You must have more questions. I have questions –'

I was already out of the door, hurrying to lose myself in the crowd.

While I'd been in the café, the stream of people going to the demo had turned into a flood. They were becoming more animated the closer we got to the temple. Strangers were shaking hands and clapping each other on the back; an occasional cheer could be heard, along with bursts of nervous laughter.

As soon as the temple loomed into view, I felt a surge of homesickness. I'd tried not to have great hopes of Harry, but the idea of not being an orphan was more seductive than I'd let myself admit. Now I knew for certain that the temple was the only home I'd ever have, even if I'd been cast out of it. Its dome shone like a pearl in the early evening sun, the gilt-tipped columns soared heavenwards. Across the pediment, the carvings of Brutus, Artemis and Herne looked both solemn and peaceful, utterly sure of their power and their place in the world.

The square was already heaving with people. The late prime minister had been widely regarded as a crook, if not a murderer, but there were still a lot of *Justice 4 Riley* signs. Most of the banners called for free elections, free speech, a free UK. Others demanded a free oracle. *Aura* IN, *Callisto* OUT. *When Artemis Speaks, Let Us Listen.*

A much smaller counter-demonstration in support of Cally had gathered at the bottom of the temple steps. Police were a heavy presence but there was no sign of the Civil Guard. Perhaps the foreign TV crews that had gathered had something to do with it. They were busy interviewing people in the crowd.

They had a wide variety to choose from. Scruffy student types, like Aiden and his activist friends. Middle-aged housewives. Veterans of the wars in the Middle East, many of whom were on crutches and in wheelchairs. Office drones, unshaven construction workers. And groups of muscular, flinty-faced young men in red or purple bandanas. The gangbangers were out too – and on a truce.

Shortly after I squeezed into the throng, a fleet of cars from the Sanctuary drove through the space cleared by the police. Veiled handmaidens and priestesses emerged to boos and jeers from the crowd. I looked for Leto's hunched figure. The handmaidens were holding hands, the little twins stumbling on their drapes as they hurried into the shelter of the temple. They must be terrified. Why was the whole cult attending a private oracle? Opis and Cally must have already made their grand entrance, for the High Priestess's gold chariot was parked at the bottom of the steps. All this pomp and ceremony seemed unnecessarily provocative.

More time passed. The shadows lengthened; the sun was a low, rich gold. The protesters weren't tiring, though.

In fact, they were only getting more energised. When Malcolm Greeve's car finally arrived, the place erupted.

I'd seen a lot of General Ferrer in the news and I could see the appeal of his firm jaw and kind eyes. His ally, and the official leader of the coup, didn't make such a good pin-up. Malcolm Greeve was just as creepy-looking as I remembered from his visits to the temple. Seb and Lionel Winter were waiting by the doors to welcome him.

The smatter of competing shouts and slogans had turned into an angry roar. 'Oracle Out! Committee Out! Free Oracle! Free UK!' The ranks of police stared on, impassive. The counter-demonstration stamped and yelled.

I shook my head, trying to clear it, and fixed my eyes on the last person I wanted to see. The only person I wanted to see.

Aiden.

At once I turned and tried to get away, but the crowd was too tightly wedged. 'You can't talk to me,' I hissed. 'You can't look at me. You can't be here. I told Scarlet to keep you away.'

'Hey – I don't need your or anyone else's permission to be here. This thing is a lot bigger than the two of us, and whatever issues we have.'

Issues? I stared at him in incomprehension. He glowered back.

'Scarlet should never have helped you leave. We could have worked it out, Aura. What the hell were you thinking, vanishing like that?'

He was angry. That was no good; I needed him to be afraid.

'I had to keep away from you for your own safety! Don't you get it? The goddess possessed *me* to punish *you*. I can't let that happen again.'

Aiden wasn't even listening. 'I was sure you'd be here,' he was saying. 'I've been looking for you in the crowd for the last hour. You can't run away this time. You have to –'

It was too much. Too much noise, too much energy and anger. The air throbbed with it. I covered my ears.

It didn't make any difference.

Artemis Selene was already here and burning through my blood. I thought my bones would crack from the force of her.

Aiden's face loomed into view, as I twisted and groaned. He was briefly replaced with gawping onlookers. 'Get back,' he shouted, pushing them off. 'It's the oracle! The true oracle. Aura, your High Priestess. Listen to her! Listen to the goddess!'

Hot tears sparked from my eyes. My body was arched like a drawn bow, pulled back to breaking point. My voice would be the arrow: shining and merciless. I begged for release. I begged the goddess to let it fly.

I was not broken, not yet.

I was not released either. Instead, I was standing in a great city, its temples and watchtowers and palaces silent and peaceful in the night. I knew, though, that their quiet was an illusion.

The moon waxed and waned. Clouds rushed over it, fog rolled through the city's streets. It stung my eyes and my lungs, bringing with it the stench of burning.

There was something dark and slick under my feet. Not oil, blood. The sky was on fire. I could hear clashes and shouts and wailing. And a voice of rage and grief in my head that wasn't my own. I stood in a shadowed colonnade and watched Troy burn, as the goddess lamented her lost city.

Torn flesh, wrecked bone.

Rubble and ash.

A city of ruins, then of wilderness – creeping weeds and brambles, tangled grasses, spindly trees. And still the keening sobs of grief in my head. Not one voice, now, but a multitude: old and young, men and women, on and on.

'For who will save the holy places? The old temple despoiled, the new one besieged. Now the iron men are on the march, and they will drag the lawmakers from the sacred altars. Alas for Troy, alas for her children –'

CHAPTER 20

My eyes snapped open. I was surrounded by a ring of strangers: tightly packed, silent, staring.

'What did I say?'

Yet the words of the prophecy were already coming back to me. This time, however, I didn't need a Lord Herne to interpret. I knew what the holy places were.

The old temple: the building we were standing in front of, where Opis and Lionel and Malcolm Greeve were busy despoiling the oracle.

The new temple: Westminster Abbey, where the rebel MPs had gathered to form an alternative government. The Gothic building wasn't 'new' in the usual sense of the word. But the Christians came after us pagans. It was new as far as Artemis was concerned.

The MPs were the lawmakers. And General Ferrer's soldiers – the iron men – were on their way to arrest them. Malcolm Greeve's visit was a deliberate distraction, designed to draw the protesters away from Parliament Square, and the real business of the day.

Voices were shouting out for news. 'What happened? What did she say? Where's the oracle?'

Aiden had a protective arm round my shoulder. I shook him off, flung back my head and gave a shout of my own.

'Westminster Abbey is under attack. The general's going to arrest our MPs. We must defend –'

The next moment, I was seized by rough hands. After a brief panicked struggle, I realised these weren't police, but supporters. A couple of men lifted me so that I stood above the crowd. My cap had fallen off so that my pale hair streamed free, my face was gilded by the dying sun. I hardly knew what I shouted: the words of the oracle, jumbled up with my own. But the goddess must have hushed the crowd, for my voice echoed around the square with uncanny strength, as if magnified by the City's stones.

Whatever I said, it was received with roars of support from my fellow citizens. I was passed above their heads as they chanted my name. 'Aura! Aura! Aura!' There was a scrimmage at the temple steps, and somehow Opis's char-iot was unhooked from its horses and dragged into the crowd. I was thrust into it, so that I stood upright at the helm, as a group of burly young men began pull it through the square.

The police were trying to contain the crowd. They had their batons out and riot shields at the ready. There were scuffles and shouts, cracked heads and bloody noses. I'd lost Aiden in the confusion until, just for a second, I thought I saw him again. He had blood on his forehead and an older woman was trying to drag him free from under the body of a fallen protester. His eyes were closed. The next moment, though, I had lost him in the crowd.

Goddess, keep him safe, I prayed. But I'd already prayed to Artemis to cut all trace of him out of my heart. She hadn't answered yet. My only comfort was that the police's efforts seemed curiously restrained. Perhaps they were inhibited by the TV cameras. Perhaps they heard the call of the goddess too.

The demonstrators poured towards Parliament Square, following the route of the Festival Day procession. I was leading the charge on my man-drawn chariot. I was jerked back and forth, trying desperately to stay upright.

Throughout the ride, I saw flashes of a different city. London, back when it was Troia Nova; when the Temple of Artemis was just one among many pagan monuments; when the city was crammed with gods now long forgotten. Their statues and shrines lining the roads, their temples crowning the hills, the smoke from a hundred sacrificial fires rising to the sky. I felt wild, loose, about to spin out of my own skin.

As the light faded, the hush of the city's traffic-free streets felt more sinister than peaceful. By the time we reached Parliament Square, the horizon was streaked with crimson. The abbey's windows glowed comfortingly, despite its crumbling carvings and soot-stained walls.

I jumped down from the chariot and ran across the green in the centre of the square. I was among the first to arrive at the abbey's doors. We were too late. The Civil Guard was already stationed there, with a couple of armoured trucks waiting outside.

As the rest of the protesters poured into the square and saw what had happened, the roar of anger seemed to split the city's skies. Rumours were flying that the army was on the way, with water cannons to disperse the crowds, troops to storm the square. A helicopter assault would land on the roof of the Houses of Parliament. Secret agents inside the abbey would machine-gun the prisoners at the general's command.

Yet nobody was going home. Instead, the abbey was quickly surrounded, Parliament Square and its exits blocked by a dense mass of people. Among them, I thought I saw faces I recognised. Mrs Galloway with her Elite Cleaning boys. Harry Soames. Spidey, from the squat. Their faces all had the same look: nervous but determined. The journalists and TV crews were there too, jostling for the best shots.

I was standing right in front of the abbey, where a line of military police had cordoned off the area between the doors and the armoured trucks. I had a self-appointed guard of my own, made up of the men who had pulled my chariot.

A couple of clergymen were the first to emerge from the abbey, hands cuffed and led by two guards. The dissident MPs followed, stumbling along in frumpy suits with shell-shocked faces. They weren't obvious hero material. But neither were we. Tonight, we were all rebels, all one. Both MPs and clergymen were greeted with a tumult of cheers.

Then the general himself came out. Crisp and upright in his uniform, every inch the born leader.

He wasn't fazed by the bellows of rage. He'd faced down worse. He stood on the steps of the abbey and surveyed the assembled mob.

He raised his hands in an appeal for calm. His voice rang out confidently. 'I am not your enemy. These people are. Greedy, lying politicians who have done their best to destroy our country. Now they have formed an illegal assembly, to undo the good work of –'

The rest of his words were shouted down. There was a smashing sound – somebody had thrown a beer bottle into the cordoned area. Somebody else threw a stone. With frightening smoothness, the Civil Guard moved into position, guns drawn.

Facing them were the gangbangers and war veterans – ex-soldiers to whom the general was just another leader out for his own ends. But there were lots of ordinary women among the front ranks of the crowd too, as well as students and the elderly. The guards might be outnumbered but we were outgunned. Would they shoot into an unarmed crowd?

And was Aiden part of it? I pushed the thought away at the same time as pushing towards the youngest guard in the line, the one with the nervous mouth. 'I want to speak to the general.'

'Let her through,' the general said.

I stepped past the guards and stood face to face with the Iron Lord.

The wild elation of the chariot ride had subsided, but the goddess was still with me. I tasted blood and ashes. I smelled charred flesh. I heard the goddess's lamentation echo from the city's stones. I was afraid of her. I was not of him.

His eyes flicked over me. 'It's the little clairvoyant,' he said with a fatherly smile. 'You should stick to palm-reading, not politics, my dear.'

'We're beyond politics. You've dragged us into war.'

'What does a girl like you know about war?' This time, he spoke with contempt.

'And what does a man like you know about keeping the peace?'

The cameras rolled, bulbs flashed.

I felt a wave of exhaustion. I was exhausted from speaking for the goddess, exhausted from keeping her at bay. I couldn't understand how I had got here. How it had come to this. I looked at the general and realised that perhaps this was true of him too. He wanted power on his own terms, but he wanted popularity too. He had been a hero for a long time. That must be hard to give up.

He narrowed his eyes. 'Your moon-lady has no power over me.'

'You're free not to believe in Artemis. That's your right. Just as we should be free to decide who we're governed by, and how. That's why you have to let these people go.'

One of the guards stepped towards me. He took my arm, and looked at the general.

The crowd raged and thundered. I barely heard them. I was waiting for what the general's order would be. He could have me put in cuffs and dragged into the truck with the other prisoners. He could have me shot where I stood. Live, on TV. There was no going back from this moment, for either of us.

For a long moment, we looked at each other. Artemis wasn't with me any more. Perhaps for the truly important moments the gods step back. They let our hearts and minds be human – nothing more or less.

Finally the general shook his head, let out a short and disbelieving laugh. I think he may even have been about to give the order to stand down. But the crowd had already lost patience. They surged towards us, a howling, rampaging tidal wave, so that everyone in front of the abbey's doors – general, soldiers, civilians – was caught up in the current. We were flung against each other and the walls, then dragged under and trampled down, then pulled up again, thrashing and breathless, fighting for air.

It was a miracle no shots were fired. Perhaps this was Artemis's doing. Perhaps it was the prayers of the Christian priests. Or maybe the soldiers just didn't get the chance.

In the end, the general and his men managed to beat a retreat to the safety of their armoured trucks. Although the mob swarmed round the vehicles, banging their fists and screaming abuse, they weren't able to topple them. The trucks stubbornly nudged their way out of the square, then sped off into the night.

Suddenly people were swarming around me too, laughing and applauding, chanting my name, plucking at my clothes and my hair. I was jostled and shaken; if one of the priests hadn't taken me under his wing, I would have fallen again. He and a fellow clergyman shepherded me into the abbey, along with some of the injured protesters, and closed the doors.

It was strange to be in such a place. All through the centuries, we'd been competing faiths, authorities, tourist attractions. I thought the abbey draughty and gloomy, and pitifully plain when compared to the temple's glitter.

Yet it was somehow also like home. There was the same smell of incense and candle smoke, the same solemn, hushed air. And the Christian priests – the dean and a canon – were kind.

They sat me down in one of the side chapels and brought me water. A couple of the MPs were there too. Like me, they were a little dazed, but soon began to regain their spirits.

'It's the beginning of the end,' said a middle-aged woman who said she was a shadow health minister. 'The Emergency Committee members are already fighting like cat and dog. After an embarrassment like this, there's no way General Ferrer can hold them together.'

'We can't be complacent,' said the dean. 'That's what got us into this mess in the first place.'

'And it was Artemis who got us out,' I said.

The clergyman gave me a wary smile. 'Faith does indeed move in mysterious ways. You were very brave to challenge the general as you did.'

I shook my head. It wasn't courage. It was the exhaustion of someone with nothing to lose. Just for a moment, part of me wouldn't have minded if the general had shot me where I stood.

A couple of medics were attending to the injured, and

now the canon went outside to appeal for any more doctors in the crowd. He came back to report that bonfires had been lit on the green, bottles were being passed around, and there was laughter and dancing. A lot of people were camped outside the main doors, waiting for me to emerge and perform miracles. One of them, he said, claimed to be a friend of mine and had left a message for me.

Aiden, I thought, with a clench of my heart. I remembered the glimpse of his bloody face, among the crush of bodies and police batons. I'd thought I'd caught sight of him urging on the crowd in the final push. But the priest said the friend was a young woman, and that her face was covered. She seemed frightened, he said.

CHAPTER 21

The note was from Cynthia, though her handwriting was so cramped it was nearly illegible. She said that she had run away from the Sanctuary just before Malcolm Greeve's visit and now she didn't know what to do or where to go. She would wait for me behind the abbey, on the corner of Solomon Street.

One of the medics agreed to be my decoy. We were about the same build and colouring. After we'd swapped clothes it wasn't a bad match, in the dark. She left through a side entrance, to draw attention away from me as I made my own exit through the back.

The streets were full of people out in defiance of the curfew, even though the telephone networks were still down and the roads closed to traffic. Some of them were heading home after the demonstration, but many others were coming to join the ongoing celebrations. The city was being reclaimed by its citizens.

Cynthia was waiting on the corner, her face part-covered by a scarf. When she saw me, she started, looked around in a panicky sort of way, and headed down the street. I called for her to wait, then reluctantly followed.

The road was well lit and there were plenty of people about. We were only a few minutes away from the abbey. Even so, I regretted turning down offers of an escort. I had been worried that the presence of strangers might alarm the fugitive.

When she turned into an alleyway, I kept my distance. I didn't like this. 'Cynthia?'

She stopped and turned. 'It's not Cynthia,' said Cally's voice from behind the scarf. 'I'm sorry –'

There was an engine's roar, squealing brakes, screeching tyres. A felt hood was already dropping over my head, as an unknown assailant pinned my arms behind my back and bundled me into a car.

My heart was speeding, a thin, dry buzz. I felt smooth leather seats, smelled the faintest trace of cigar smoke and perfume. I thought I might be in one of the Trinovantum Council's limos, the ones with blacked-out windows, and a pass for the curfew. After only a short drive – at high speed – the car came to an abrupt halt, and I was marched along the pavement, then down a steep flight of stairs.

A trickle of sweat ran down my back. I had already guessed where I was being taken. Then I smelled smoke and herbs and knew for certain.

Sure enough, when my hood was removed, I found myself standing in the Chamber of the Oracle. There was Artemis Selene in her alcove. There was the tripod seat and brazier on the stand. There was the little bronze door.

And there, standing in the lamplight and flickering shadows, were the people who'd tried to steal the oracle from me. Seb and Lionel Winter looked out of place in their suits, but Opis and Cally more than made up for it in their ritual finery. Malcolm Greeve had clearly been given the full show.

Opis was wearing the moonstone headdress, her white robes overlaid with a silver brocade mantel studded with pearls. She looked like a column of ice. Cally was swathed in purple-black drapes, presumably for dramatic contrast. Her hair was coiffured into an elaborate crown of curls, her face heavily made up with glittering eyelids and a glossy red mouth. She regarded me steadily but with no sign of recognition.

The two priestesses and the Lord Herne had the slightly smudged, tousled appearance of people who've stayed too long at a party. Lionel Winter was plucking irritably at his lip; Cally's face was wan and pinched under the heavy cosmetics. Only Seb seemed untouched, his bronze helmet of hair smooth as ever, his face a perfectly regular blank. It must have been him who'd bundled me into the car; now he busied himself with binding my wrists and legs. He gave a little smirk, and I wondered how I'd ever thought him handsome.

'What have you done to Cynthia?' I asked, though my mouth was so dry it was hard to speak.

'You needn't concern yourself with her,' said Opis. 'She and Leto have transgressed, and they will be punished appropriately. Your crimes, however, are of a more grievous nature. You have sinned against Holy Artemis in thought, word and deed. And her judgement shall be merciless.'

Cally made a small muffled sound. Seb took her hand and patted it soothingly.

'I'm not worried about the goddess,' I said. 'I've kept my vows – unlike everyone else in this room.'

'Do you have any idea what you've done, girl?' Lionel Winter's eyes were rimmed with red and his pale sweep of hair was looking dishevelled rather than majestic. 'Until recently, it's true, you might have led a sheltered life, but I can't believe you are ignorant of what's become of this country. The poverty, the squalor, the chaos. The people have been crying out for leadership. Somebody had to step in. Somebody had to take charge. Yet you've done nothing but undermine the authority of our new government and incite rebellion. We are doing this for the good –'

'No. You're doing this out of vanity and greed.' I looked at Opis. 'You can't still believe that I'm making the prophecies up. Aren't you even a *little* afraid of what you're doing?'

Cally made another choking noise.

'Sebastian, take Callisto out of here,' Opis said sharply. 'The poor girl's getting upset.'

Seb put his arm round Callisto's shoulders, whispered tenderly in her ear. Then he led her by the hand up the stairs to the Sacred Hall. She didn't look back.

'What a lovely couple,' I said. 'Your pimping has really paid off. The two of you must be very proud.'

Lionel looked genuinely offended. 'I am a sanctified person and loyal servant of the goddess. Everything I have done, for the cult and the country, has been in good faith.'

'Yes, you little slut,' Opis hissed. 'Don't think we don't know what you've been up to with that lout Aiden Carlyle –'

Lionel gave a slight cough. 'My dear, perhaps we should stay focused on the issue at hand. If Aura is to publicly renounce her oracles –'

'That's all very well. But first Aura needs to atone for her transgressions.'

I swallowed hard. Lionel and Opis were looking at each other, in silent negotiation.

'Your time will come later, Lionel,' she said. 'For now, this is a disciplinary matter between Aura and me. And Holy Artemis.'

He seemed about to object, but Opis drew herself up to her full height. 'I am still High Priestess and head of this temple. There are rituals to be performed, penance to be made. I will exorcise Aura's demons and lead her back to the path of righteousness. You need to leave me to my work.'

The Lord Herne didn't look happy. But he did, in the end, turn and go.

And then it was just me and Opis, alone in the underworld.

*   *   *

For a long time neither of us spoke. I looked past Opis to the small crude statue of the goddess. If one could see behind the carved veil, I thought she would be smiling, curved and secret and cold, colder than stone.

'I can feel her,' I said. 'Artemis. She's with us now. Watching, waiting.'

'You're lying.'

'I'm not. And neither was my mother, Carya. Yes – I know the truth about her now. Harry Soames told me everything.'

'Your mother was a lying slut. Just like you.'

'Her oracle was true, and so are mine.'

'Shut up.' Opis thrust her head forward. Just for a moment, I thought I saw a forked tongue flicker from her mouth. 'Shut up.' She took a step back, gave a cracked laugh. 'Funny. I used to think you were such a poor mousy little thing. Not like Carya, who was always so full of herself, so insolent, though she came from nothing. Sly too. She'd bat her eyes at every man who crossed her path, worming her way into their affections. Even after I'd won, and I'd taken my rightful place at the head of the cult, she was scheming to undermine me. Steal what was *mine*.' Flecks of spit had gathered in the corner of Opis's mouth; her make-up was smeared all around her eyes. I had never seen her less than perfectly polished, in perfect control. This was much more frightening.

'It didn't take long for Carya's crimes to be exposed. By attempting to steal the position from me, that whore brought shame upon herself and the temple, and the goddess took her revenge. And I was generous in my victory. I gave her bastard a home. I gave you food, clothes, an education. You wanted for nothing. And then – *then* – you flung it all back in my face. Trying to mock me, to ruin me. Just as Carya had. You see, I know what you are. Like mother, like daughter. Yes. *You* are the real snake in this temple.'

I licked my dry lips. 'Everything . . . everything I have done has been for the goddess.'

'Oh? Then where is she now? If she's watching, waiting, why isn't she coming to rescue you?' Opis flung out her arms. 'Where is her thunderbolt, her silver arrow?'

Her laughter echoed around the crypt. Her smile was like ice.

'You've forgotten the stories I raised you on, Aura. The gods are no better than us. Unfaithful, neglectful. Cruel. I think you are alone. I think you are all alone, with me.'

I braced myself for some act of violence. The High Priestess, however, had a ritual to prepare. She moved away from me with an impatient whisk of her skirts and set about lighting two black candles in the statue's alcove. They had been studded with animal teeth. As the candles melted, fragments of yellowed fangs were released into pools of wax.

Opis held up a small gong and began to beat it rhythmically as she circled the brazier, pausing now and then to toss yew berries on to the dish of herbs above the fire. A purplish, sickly-sweet smoke soon filled the room. The shuddering clash of the gong pulsed in my head, so I could hardly hear the High Priestess's chant. I knew what it was, though: the words of a casting-out ceremony. *Where there is Light, let there be Dark; where there is Hope, Dread; where there is Love, Loss* . . .

As the last quivers of the gong died away, Opis took out a small clay doll and a spool of black twine. Still chanting, she slowly wound the twine around the manikin. The words she was now saying were nonsense, mainly: a curse so ancient that most of the meaning was lost, fragments of Greek and Latin mixed with Arabic. Once the doll was entirely mummified in thread, she placed it in a small lead casket and shut the lid with a snap.

Her voice shook with a kind of fearful triumph.

'Aura of the Cult of Artemis, you have betrayed your vows, made on the stones of Troy and the blood of Brutus.

The Holy Lady of the Moon, Queen of Beasts, has set your punishment. I, as her High Priestess, must seal your fate.'

With that, Opis kicked the back of my knees so that I fell to the floor, forced into a clumsy bow to the goddess.

'That's right. Kneel before our Holy Lady. Ask her forgiveness. Beg for mine. You sought refuge in the temple of the Christian priests. But I, too, can give you communion.'

She had the gold chalice from King Brutus's altar. I clamped my mouth shut but it wasn't any good. She pinched my nose so I couldn't breathe, and forced the hard rim of the cup between my lips. My lips stung and bled; I thought my teeth would crack. The drug wasn't disguised by spiced wine this time. It was bitter and acrid and burned my throat. I coughed and spluttered as forcefully as I could, but some of the liquid still went down.

'Where is the goddess now?' Opis called. 'Where has she gone?' Her jagged laughter rocked around me as the world shattered into black.

CHAPTER 22

I slipped in and out of a sickly consciousness. I was swimming in the pool at Rick Moodie's house, trying to catch my breath in between crashing waves of blackness. I was lying in the wood, among dead leaves, as the earth quaked with serpents. Cally had locked me in the wardrobe again and was rocking, rocking it . . .

When I regained consciousness, the ground was still and the air was dark.

My muscles felt like cotton wool. My legs were scraped, my clothes damp with mud. My ears still seemed to ring with the crashing of the gong.

For a long moment I blinked about with bewilderment. A small, hopeless part of me clung to the idea that I was in the grip of a hallucination. I put my hands out, brushed smooth stone to either side. Staggering to my bruised knees, I stretched my hands upwards, and touched something else cold and solid. Iron.

That ringing in my ears – it wasn't the echo of the gong. It was the slamming down of an iron lid. The lid that sealed me into my tomb.

Frantically, I scrubbed at my eyes. The blindness, some after-effect of the drug, was lifting and I saw there was light in here, after all. The flickering of a small oil lamp revealed that I was in a circular stone well, just over a metre wide and two metres deep. The only furnishings were the lamp and a knife.

I bent double and began to retch.

I wasn't in the Place of Punishment that Cally and I had been taken to visit. That was a sunken chamber, on a small hill in the centre of the cult cemetery. These days, it was fenced off with iron bars and left open to the elements. I must be in a secret back-up option. Somewhere I would never be found. The thought sent me retching again. It felt like my guts were being scraped up from my stomach.

Opis . . . Callisto . . . Aiden . . . Artemis. Maybe the goddess had meant for this to happen all along – ever since I'd kissed Aiden in the woods. Maybe this had always been my destiny.

In the sickly glow of the lamp, I saw scratch marks on

the walls. It looked like someone had clawed at them with their nails. Other women and girls had died here. I could smell their fear, their thirst and their hunger, sweating out from the stones. How many agonised hours, days, had it taken before they were released into death?

But I wouldn't have to wait.

Opis had untied my hands and given me the means to end it quickly. In that, she had been merciful.

The ancient Greeks didn't spend much time speculating about the afterlife. The Elysian Fields are where the heroes go; Tartarus is for those who deserve the torments of hell. The details on both are vague. And when I tried to visualise Elysium, I could only imagine a larger-scale version of Artemisia House. An eternity spent wandering around gilded columns and faded tapestries. An eternity populated with stone heroes and taxidermy animals, brought back to a dusty half-life.

Do you vow to honour the laws of the temple and this land? Opis had asked me once.

I *do*, I had answered, *lest I suffer the arrows of Artemis and the waters of the Styx.*

Styx, the river of hate. It was one of five rivers in the underworld. Rivers of pain, of fire, of wailing and of forgetfulness.

Forgetfulness. That's what I wanted. I thought what it must mean, to be unfurled out of my body and out of the world, pitched into oblivion. After all, only a few hours ago I had been ready for death. I had wanted to be free. It was the price I had been willing to pay for being released from the goddess.

Well, Artemis had taken me at my word. I had rejected her and so she had left me. Opis was right: I was alone.

The stone walls seemed to close round me, squeezing out the air. Electricity sparked along every nerve, my heart bucked in my chest. I began to fancy I couldn't breathe, even as the first scream raced through my veins, exploded up through my body. My voice howled, raw and animal, in the stone cell. On and on and on and on. The silence afterwards was like falling into another pit.

The lamp wouldn't burn for much longer. I didn't want to die in the dark. Most of all, I didn't want to die alone. I wanted the goddess to be with me. I took up the knife. It was thin and razor-sharp. I fixed my eyes on the lamp. I took deep, shaky breaths.

Goddess. Holy Mother. Queen. I am yours. I have always been yours, now and forever. Forgive me, be merciful.

I closed my eyes. The blade of the knife grazed my

chest, like the tip of the silver arrow at my initiation, a lifetime ago.

Come back to me, Holy Artemis. Have mercy upon me. Have mercy . . .

And, at the end, the goddess listened. A chime, unearthly sweet, shook the air, and the breath of soft laugher brushed against my spine. I heard a dog howl.

The wild hunt was coming for me, to take me to Elysium.

The blade pricked my skin. It would be the bite of a hound, sharp teeth ripping through my body and seizing my soul, dragging me into the afterlife –

The dog barked again. Rough, urgent. Familiar.

I opened my eyes. The lamp had gone out. Darkness pressed all around me, thick as fear, heavy as stone. I shouldn't be able to hear anything through that iron lid. Yet a dog had barked, and I had heard it. A flesh-and-blood bark. A bark from the ordinary world.

I tried to shout. It was hopeless – my voice was rubbed raw from screaming. All I could manage was a hoarse whisper.

Yet the dog answered me. It barked on and on, then began to whine. The whining turned into a creak. The creak got louder. With a rusty, straining sound, the iron lid inched upwards.

I saw a grey wolfhound, its panting breath steaming joyously in the night air. I saw Cally, crying. And Aiden, saying my name, over and over, like an answered prayer.

And then he was there, with me, in the pit, and we were clutching each other like we had in the wood, entangled, pulling at each other's clothes, grasping at each other's hair. His skin was warm bronze, and my tears and his were salt, running through my hair, down my neck, through our entwined hands.

CHAPTER 23

It was Cally, however, who had led the rescue.

'I told Lionel you were his daughter,' was how she began.

'*What?*' Even after everything that had happened in the last few hours, this made me start.

She nodded. We were walking through the cult cemetery, in which my tomb had been one of thousands. Row upon row of identical black stone urns. The names carved on the urns were identical too. I had already seen three Auras, two Caryas and an Opis.

The urns didn't interest me, however. I kept looking from Cally to Aiden and back again. I wanted to keep touching them, to check they were real. Cally's revelation, however, had jolted me out of my dreamlike state.

'It's silly,' she said, 'but I got the idea because you and Lionel both do that thing with your lip. You know – pulling at it when you're nervous or worried about something. Well, Lionel was doing it when we were in the Chamber of the Oracle, and I remembered it's something I always associate with you. And you do have the same sort of colouring.'

Aiden and I both started to object.

'It wasn't just the physical stuff,' Cally said calmly. 'It was more about how Opis talked about Carya . . .'

After Seb had ushered Cally out of the crypt, they were supposed to go back to the Sanctuary. But she was desperate to know what Opis had planned for me. So outside the temple, she told him she'd lost an earring, and wanted to return to the Sacred Hall to look for it. When she saw Lionel leaving, she hid behind a pillar, then sneaked back downstairs.

'You see, Opis had already told me what happened with your mother and Harry Soames. She said it was proof of how you were lying about the oracle, and why Mr Soames had made those accusations at the festival. She said you were bad blood and cursed by the goddess. But when she got you alone in the crypt, and was so wild and ranting . . . so jealous of Carya, after all these years . . . that's when I thought that maybe their rivalry was about love as well as power. And not for Harry, but Lionel.'

My mother had chosen the wrong man to love, and it had resulted in hate. A hate that had poisoned Opis, and nearly killed me.

I had thought the worst of my fears and regrets had been left behind in the pit. Now I realised this wasn't true. Yet I couldn't give in to them. I mustn't let the poison spread.

'How much else did you hear?' I asked Cally laboriously.

'Not much. Seb came to find me, just as Opis kicked you to the floor. He forced me back to the High Priestess's residence, to wait with him and Lionel.

'Lionel was really tense. The communications network was back up, and his phone was going crazy. What happened with the general in Parliament Square had really rattled him. The plan was to force you to publicly renounce your oracles on TV. They were going to blackmail you, you see, because they've got Cynthia and Leto locked up somewhere in the Sanctuary.

'But Opis had told them they didn't need blackmail, and that if she could just get you on your own she could make you see the error of your ways. I don't think Seb and Lionel knew what she was planning. I'd guessed, though. I had heard it in her voice.

'Suddenly I snapped. I couldn't understand what had

happened to me. Why I was just sitting there, in my ridiculous costume, like a little doll. I was just a toy to them. To everyone. So I got up and said I was going to find you. They tried to stop me leaving, and – and I kicked Seb. Between the legs. Hard.'

I laughed then, in spite of everything.

'Attagirl,' said Aiden.

Cally gave a small bleak smile. 'That's when I told Lionel you were his daughter. He was so shocked he just stood there, blinking and spluttering. He kept saying no, you were a boy, and you were dead. I ran past him and he didn't stop me either.'

Cally had fled to the Sanctuary gates. Another Trinovantum Council car was outside, ready for when the Winters wanted to leave. She got in and told the driver she had an urgent errand. He was surprised, but she was the oracle, all dressed up in her ritual finery, and so he did as he was told. Only a few minutes later, she saw Aiden among a group of protesters heading towards the temple. She ordered the driver out, and Aiden in.

The two of them then drove to the cemetery. 'I had this gut instinct that Opis would take you to the Place of Punishment,' Cally said. 'And then we saw one of her pearl hairpins lying on the ground by the gates, so we knew we were on the right track. But this place is huge. We didn't know where to start – until Argos bounded out of the bushes. We all thought he was on the run with you. But it was like he'd been waiting for us the whole time.'

Argos licked my hand and wagged his tail. He must have been living rough ever since I lost him outside the squat, but although he was thinner, and there were burrs in his coat, he showed no ill effects from his adventures.

The lid of my prison had been covered in grass matting, and there was a black urn on the top, just like all the other graves. The lid itself was closed with an ordinary bolt, which had been recently oiled. Opis had made her preparations well. If it hadn't been for Argos, I would never have been found.

As we approached the cemetery gates, Aiden and I hung back, our hands just touching.

'Don't disappear again,' he said.

Argos woofed, as if in agreement. I took a deep breath.

'Artemis was with me in the pit, just like she was with me and you in the woods. She's still with me,' I told him. 'Still *in* me. I can feel it. Do you . . . do you understand?'

'I do.'

We walked on in silence. There was dried blood on his forehead from his assault at the protest. He looked like he'd slept in his clothes, his hair was dirty and his nails were bitten down to the quick. I had never seen anything so beautiful in my life. Beautiful, and forbidden.

Cally was waiting for us by the car. Just before we got there, Aiden came to an abrupt stop. He spoke quickly, with irritable little tugs at his hair. 'OK. Here's the thing. I just want you to know that I'm with you too. As well as the goddess. I won't ask you for anything, I won't get in your way. But I'll be here, Aura, for as long as you need me. OK?'

I tried to smile, even though a shadow had passed over my heart. The small black urns had reminded me of the Sibyl in her jar. He had made a noble gesture, but it wouldn't work in the real world. Not as long as Artemis had me in her grip. Until I was free, neither was Aiden.

In the meantime, we needed to find Lionel. Only he could put a stop to Opis. 'I wouldn't be surprised if she has a get-out plan,' Aiden said. 'She might already be on a jet to some tropical island hideaway.'

'She'll be wherever the Lord Herne is,' said Cally. She squeezed my hand. 'I'm sorry about Lionel. I . . . well . . . I know what it's like, having a parent who isn't up to much. But at least he didn't know who you were.'

I squeezed Cally's hand back. I decided that my mother had been right: I was a child of the goddess. Lionel Winter was not, and would never be, a part of my true self.

Aiden parked a little way from the Sanctuary. We thought we would start our search there, but then we saw that all the temple lights were blazing.

Quite a few people were milling about in the square, even though it was midnight. A group had set up camp, ready for another day of protests. When we were recognised – the two rival oracles, arm in arm – there was quite a commotion. However, thanks to Cally's set of keys, we were up the steps and through the temple doors before anyone could waylay us.

The Sacred Hall was lit up like on Festival Day. Bundles of lilies were everywhere; the smell was overpoweringly sweet. The altar itself was a mess. Among a clutter of amulets was a bowl of salt and a white dove, its entrails spilled on to a gold dish.

Aiden frowned. 'What the hell . . . ?'

'It's the remnants of a purification ritual. For atonement,' Cally replied.

I raised my brows. 'Maybe our Honoured Lady isn't so sure she's immune from thunderbolts after all.'

'So where is she now?' asked Aiden.

Cally pointed to the door leading to the crypt. It was ajar.

Aiden wanted to go first, but I wouldn't let him. I wasn't afraid. I didn't think I'd be afraid ever again. I had already been to the underworld and back today.

The three of us crept down the worn stone steps. There was no door at the bottom so I hung back in the shadows of the stairwell.

I heard Lionel's voice, ragged with barely suppressed fury. 'How dare you keep this from me? My own flesh and blood –'

'Why would you care?' Opis spat back. 'She was under your nose the whole time. But you didn't look. You didn't want to know. Just like you didn't want to know about Carya. You believed what you wanted to, like always.'

'You lied to me. You tricked me. Carya –'

'Carya was an even bigger fool than me. You played us both. The best years of my life I've given to you, and this cult. And what do I get for it? What do I have? Nothing and no one.'

'Oh, please. Even now, you reek with ambition. I never wanted to involve the oracle in the coup. I did it to please you.'

'And you've managed to screw that up too, along with everything else.'

'What have you done with my daughter, you bitch?'

Opis began to laugh. 'So it's different, is it, now that she's not somebody else's bastard, some faceless temple brat? You should thank me for clearing up your mess. She's in Elysium, Lionel. The goddess took her –'

I stepped out of the shadows. 'But then she brought me back.'

Opis whipped round. Her tendrils of uncombed hair seemed to lift from her head, black and snaky. Her eyes were bloodshot slits. She hissed, and her tongue flickered.

Lionel's face was all bones. 'Aura,' he said wonderingly.

Opis gave a strangled cry, and snatched up the ceremonial silver arrow that was lying on the altar. She rushed towards me, its point aimed like a dagger to my heart.

There was a loud crack. The stone room echoed with it. Opis bent over, clutching her side. There was a hole in it, bubbling and red. Behind her, Lionel was holding a pistol. His hand shook.

Opis staggered, fell, clawed at the altar. Slowly, painfully, she dragged herself on to it. She made a faint mewing sound. 'God . . .' she started to say. 'God . . .' Blood frothed out of her mouth. She let out a long, whispering sigh.

I went to her then, in spite of myself. But her eyes were already glazed.

'It's over.'

'Yes,' my father said. He nodded slowly. 'Yes, it's all over. Too late.' He gave a wry half-smile. 'The police will be here soon. I called them, to take her away. Now they will come for me.'

He looked at me carefully, searchingly, in the way Harry Soames had. Looking for traces of my mother's face, or his own.

'I'm sorry,' he said formally. 'I loved her, you see.'

I didn't know whether he meant my mother or Opis. I never will. This time, his hand didn't shake. He put the gun to his head and pulled the trigger.

I don't remember much about what happened immediately afterwards. I heard somebody sobbing; I think it was Cally. Aiden put his arms round me and I barely noticed. Then more people arrived, in uniform, and there was more commotion and shouting and bright lights. It meant nothing to me. I couldn't take my eyes off the body of the High Priestess, slumped across King Brutus's altar stone.

Blood, especially the blood of a priestess, is a powerful thing. Sacrifice calls the goddess to us. It releases her too.

My head chimed, cold and sweet. And despite the noise and confusion, the blood-spattered horror of it all, I felt a loosening deep within me. I was slack as an unstrung bow.

It was over, and I was free.

EPILOGUE

I gave my final oracle two weeks later. It was my first and last fake.

Live on TV, I rode from the Sanctuary to the temple in the High Priestess's gold chariot, through cheering crowds. I was crowned with the moonstone headdress and dressed in robes the colour of sea-foam with a girdle of amethysts. Lilies and amaranths were thrown in my path. As the handmaidens sang the processional hymn, I walked through the Sacred Hall and descended to the crypt. There I lit the candles on King Brutus's altar, and drew back the curtain to the Chamber of the Oracle.

I sat on the tripod seat and contemplated the statue in the alcove. I prayed to Holy Artemis, Lady of the Moon, Queen of Beasts, to approve my words.

Then I gave my oracle to Harry Soames, the new Lord Herne.

The oracle was long and digressive. It quoted from Homer, Euripides and Rilke. You can read the full text, along with those of my other prophecies, in the display room in the cult archive.

The references may have been rambling, but the interpretation was clear. There was no place for the army in government. The principal evildoers within the cult had been purged, but much work remained to be done and we, the people of Britain, must remain vigilant. Reform must start with free and fair elections. And a new era called for a new oracle. My service to the goddess was done.

Afterwards, I put away the headdress and the jewelled girdle, the floral wreaths. I went back to Artemisia House and signed the papers formally releasing me from the cult.

Leto is High Priestess now. She's the oldest on record, but in spite of her grumbles I reckon she'll be going strong for a good few years yet. At least until one of the younger ones is ready to step in.

Perhaps it will be Cynthia. After a lot of thought, she decided she wanted to remain in the cult and has taken charge of its new community outreach programme – hospice work and soup kitchens and battered women's shelters. The last time I visited she was almost like the girl I remembered, the girl with the dancing eyes.

Cally, though, has gone. I was the first person she told. We sat side by side in our bedroom, holding hands, in a way we'd never done even when we were little girls. Her voice faltered as she asked, 'Do you think Artemis will forgive me?'

'Of course. You were a victim in all of this too.'

'Not at first, I wasn't. It was exciting, all the attention and the fuss. All the people bringing me presents and compliments, telling me how special I was. How I'd been Chosen. And I did feel Chosen, to begin with. By Opis and Lionel and . . . and Seb.'

She winced. 'Aura,' she whispered, 'I'm so ashamed. I just . . . I'd never felt that way about anyone before. It was overwhelming. And Seb said he felt the same, and that Artemis wanted the two of us to be together. That we had a special responsibility. Opis and the Lord Herne kept saying what a terrible state the country was in, and how my oracles could bring new believers to the cult, and help restore order . . . They brought my mother in, too, and she was so proud. So excited for me. Yet I knew it was wrong, inside. And it got more wrong as time went on. But I was trapped, because I'd agreed to the lies. I just had to keep on lying.'

'How do you feel about Seb now?'

'That I wish I'd kicked him harder.' She lifted her chin, with a flash of the old Cally. I knew then that she'd be all right.

She's touring the States now, to promote a book about her time as the fake oracle. Noah Evans, Rick Moodie's agent, is representing her. He reckons she's going to go far. Cousin Seb, meanwhile, has also left the country, though in much murkier circumstances. There's a warrant out for his arrest.

The Emergency Committee didn't survive Lionel Winter's death. He was too important a figure within the coup, and his and Opis's murder–suicide was too huge a scandal to be covered up. Despite General Ferrer's efforts, the committee had already lost the support of the army, and soon collapsed in disarray. Most of its members are in prison now, awaiting trial.

The woman I met in Westminster Abbey, the one-time shadow health minister, is acting prime minister. She's got her work cut out. There are still protests and strikes, hardly any money, not enough jobs. Yet we came back from the brink, and – goddess willing – things won't get so bad again.

After my last oracle, I left the city. Aiden had helped me leave the cult, and now he was helping me build a new life, for the two of us. We spent some time on a faraway island, where there was sunshine and sand dunes and nobody had heard of Artemis, let alone me. When I came back, Harry Soames had strong-armed the Trinovantum Council to come up with the funds for a new home. I even have a new name, which took a bit of getting used to. Aiden helped pick it out.

I have never felt the goddess again. I still listen for her, under autumn trees in a gathering darkness, when the sky is streaked with gold. Or else it will be a night when the moon is bright as ice, and a dog howls into the wind. Once you have experienced the divine as a living presence, once you've known the beauty and terror of their touch, the ordinary world can seem a pale and faded thing. Only sometimes, though. And not for long.

Once, all I ever wanted was to be Chosen. But it's far better, in the end, to choose.

AUTHOR'S NOTE

Up until the sixteenth century, the story of King Brutus that Opis relates in Chapter One of this book was widely believed to be historical fact. The source for this was Geoffrey of Monmouth's *History of the Kings of Britain*, written circa 1136. Geoffrey claimed to have uncovered the true story of the founding of Britain in an ancient manuscript given to him by Walter Mapes, Archdeacon of Oxford. It is unknown what became of the manuscript, if it ever existed.

The London Stone, sometimes called the Stone of Brutus, is a block of limestone set within an iron grille on Cannon Street, in the City of London. Although its origins are obscure, legend has it that it was brought by Brutus from Troy to be the altar in the Temple of Diana (Artemis) in his new capital. According to superstition, as long as the stone is safe the city is too.

The Cult of Artemis is inspired by Greek mythology and the practices of the Vestal Virgins in Rome. The punishment for a Vestal Virgin who broke her vows was to be buried alive in the Campus Sceleratus or 'Evil Field'.

You can see Titian's painting *The Death of Actaeon* in the National Gallery in London.

ACKNOWLEDGEMENTS

I would like to thank Ellen Holgate for her heroically patient and perceptive editing, Natalie Hamilton for some very clever suggestions, and Isabel Ford and Clare Balham for their eagle-eyes.

Also by Laura Powell

'It's got witches, it's got mafia-esque rival
gangs and a gorgeous boy or two.
What more could a girl ask for?'
The Overflowing Library